# Nazi Literature
## in
## the Americas

# ROBERTO BOLAÑO

# NAZI LITERATURE IN THE AMERICAS

Translated from the Spanish by CHRIS ANDREWS

A NEW DIRECTIONS BOOK

Published by arrangement with Agencia Literaria Carmen Balcells, the Heirs of Roberto Bolaño, and Anagrama Editorial.

Manufactured in the United States of America
New Directions Books are printed on acid-free paper.
First published as a New Directions Book in 2008
Published simultaneously in Canada by Penguin Books Canada Ltd.

Library of Congress Cataloging-in-Publication Data

Bolaño, Roberto, 1953–2003.
    [Historia de la literatura Nazi en America. English]
    Nazi literature in the Americas / Roberto Bolaño ; translated into English by Chris Andrews.
        p. cm.
    ISBN 978-0-8112-1705-7 (cloth )
    ISBN 978-0-8112-1705-1 (paper)
    I. Andrews, Chris, 1962–   II. Title.
PQ8098.12.O38H5713 2007
863'.64—dc22

                                    2007037800

New Directions Books are published for James Laughlin
by New Directions Publishing Corporation,
80 Eighth Avenue, New York 10011

for Carolina López

# CONTENTS

If the flow is slow enough and you have a good bicycle, or a horse, it *is* possible to bathe twice (or even three times, should your personal hygiene so require) in the same river.

Augusto Monterroso

# THE MENDILUCE CLAN

## EDELMIRA THOMPSON DE MENDILUCE

*Buenos Aires, 1894–Buenos Aires, 1993*

At fifteen, Edelmira Thompson published her first book, *To Daddy*, which earned her a modest place in the vast gallery of lady poets active in Buenos Aires high society. And from then on, she was a regular presence in the salons of Ximena San Diego and Susana Lezcano Lafinur, dictators of taste in poetry, and of taste in general, on both banks of the Río de la Plata at the dawn of the twentieth century. Her first poems, as one might reasonably have guessed, were concerned with filial piety, religious meditation and gardens. She flirted with the idea of taking the veil. She learned to ride.

In 1917 she met the rancher and entrepreneur Sebastian Mendiluce, twenty years her senior. Everyone was surprised when they announced their engagement, after only a few months. According to people who knew him at the time, Mendiluce thought little of literature in general and poetry in particular, had no artistic sensibility (although he did occasionally go to the opera), and his conversation was on a par with that of his farmhands and factory workers. He was tall and energetic, but not handsome by any means. There was, however, no disputing his inexhaustible wealth.

Edelmira Thompson's friends considered it a marriage of convenience, but in fact she married for love. A love that neither she nor Mendiluce was ever able to explain and which endured imperturbably all the days of her life.

Marriage, which ends the careers of so many promising women writers, quickened the pen of Edelmira Thompson. She established a salon in Buenos Aires to rival those of the redoubtable Ximena San Diego and Susana Lezcano Lafinur. She took young Argentinean painters under her wing, not only buying their work (in 1950 her collection of paintings and sculptures was, if not the best in the Republic, certainly one of the largest and most extravagant), but also inviting them to paint at her ranch in Azul, far from the madding crowd, all expenses paid. She founded a publishing house, The Lamp of the South, which brought out more than fifty books of poetry, many of which were dedicated to Edelmira herself, "the fairy godmother of Argentinean letters."

In 1921 she published her first book of prose, *All My Life*, an idyllic and rather flat autobiography, devoid of gossip, full of landscapes and poetic meditations. Contrary to the author's expectations, it disappeared from the bookshop windows in Buenos Aires without leaving so much as a ripple. Disappointed, Edelmira set off for Europe with her two small sons, two servants, and more than twenty suitcases.

She visited Lourdes and the great cathedrals. She had an audience with the Pope. A yacht took her from island to island in the Aegean. She reached Crete one midday in spring. In 1922, in Paris, she published a book of children's verse in French, and another in Spanish. Then she returned to Argentina.

But things had changed, and Edelmira did not feel at ease in her country. Her new book of poems (*European Hours*, 1923) was described in a local newspaper as "precious." The nation's most influential reviewer, Dr. Enrique Belmar, described her as "an idle, childish lady whose time and energy would be better spent on good works, such as educating all the ragged little rascals on the loose throughout this vast land of ours." Edelmira's elegant reply consisted of an invitation to attend her salon, addressed to Belmar and other critics, which was ignored by all but four half-starved gossip columnists and crime reporters. Humiliated, she retired to her ranch in Azul, accompanied by a faithful few. Soothed by the rural calm and the conversations of simple, hardworking country folk, she set to work on the new book of poetry that was to be her vindication. *Argentinean Hours* (1925) sparked scandal and controversy from the day of its publication. In her new poems, Edelmira renounced contemplative vision in favor of pugnacious action. She attacked Argentina's critics and literary ladies, the decadence besetting the nation's cultural life. She argued for a return to origins: agrarian labor and the still-wild southern frontier. Flirting and swooning were behind her now. Edelmira longed for the epic and its proportions, a literature unafraid to face the challenge of singing the fatherland. One way and another, the book was a great success, but, demonstrating her humility, Edelmira barely took the time to relish her triumph, and soon left for Europe once again. She was accompanied by her children, her servants, and the

Buenos Aires philosopher Aldo Carozzone, who acted as her personal secretary.

She spent the year 1926 traveling in Italy with her numerous entourage. In 1927, she was joined by Mendiluce. In 1928, her first daughter, Luz, a bouncing, ten-pound baby, was born in Berlin. The German philosopher Haushofer was godfather to the child, and the baptism, attended by the cream of the German and Argentinean intelligentsia, was followed by three days of non-stop festivities, which culminated in a little wood near Rathenow, where the Mendiluces treated Haushofer to a kettledrum solo composed and performed by maestro Tito Vásquez, who went on to become a sensation.

In 1929, the stock-market crash obliged Sebastian Mendiluce to return to Argentina. Meanwhile Edelmira and her children were presented to Adolf Hitler, who held Luz and said, "She certainly is a wonderful little girl." Photos were taken. The future Führer of the Reich made a great impression on the Argentinean poet. Before leaving, she presented him with several of her own books and a deluxe edition of *Martin Fierro*. Hitler thanked her warmly, beseeching her to translate one of her poems into German on the spot, a task which, with the help of Carozzone, she managed to accomplish. Hitler was clearly delighted. The lines were resounding and looked to the future. In high spirits, Edelmira asked for the Führer's advice: which would be the most appropriate school for her sons? He recommended a Swiss boarding school, but added that the best school was life itself. By the end of the audience, Edelmira and Carozzone were committed Hitlerites.

1930 was a year of voyages and adventures. Accompanied by Carozzone, her young daughter (the boys were boarding at an exclusive school in Berne) and her two Indian servants, Edelmira traveled up and down the Nile, visited Jerusalem (where she had a mystical experience or a nervous breakdown, which confined her to a hotel bed for three days), then Damascus, Baghdad . . .

Her head was buzzing with projects: she planned to launch a new publishing house back in Buenos Aires, which would specialize in translations of European thinkers and novelists; she dreamed of studying architecture and designing grandiose schools to be built in parts of the country as yet untouched by civilization; she wanted to set up a foundation in memory of her mother, with the mission of helping young women from poor backgrounds to fulfill their artistic aspirations. And little by little a new book began to take shape in her mind.

In 1931 she returned to the Argentinean capital and began to carry out her projects. She launched a magazine, *Modern Argentina*, edited by Carozzone, whose mission was to publish the latest in poetry and fiction, but also political commentary, philosophical essays, film reviews, and articles on social issues. Half of the first number was devoted to Edelmira's book *The New Spring*, which came out simultaneously. Part travel narrative, part philosophical memoir, the book reflected on the state of the world, and the destinies of Europe and America in particular, while warning of the threat that Communism posed to Christian civilization.

The following years were rich and productive: she wrote new books, made new friends, traveled to new places (touring the north of Argentina, she crossed the Bolivian border on horseback), launched new publishing ventures, and diversified her artistic activity, writing the libretto for an opera (*Ana, the Peasant Redeemed*, 1935, whose première at the Teatro Colón divided the public and led to verbal and physical confrontations), painting a series of landscapes in the province of Buenos Aires, and collaborating in the production of three plays by the Uruguayan author Wenceslao Hassel.

When Sebastian Mendiluce died, in 1940, Edelmira was unable to travel to Europe, as she would have wished, because of the war. Deranged by sorrow, she composed a death notice which took up a whole page in each of the nation's major newspapers, and was signed: Edelmira, the widow Mendiluce. The text no doubt reflected her unstable mental state. It was widely mocked and derided among the Argentinean intelligentsia.

Once again, she withdrew to her ranch in Azul, accompanied only by her daughter, the faithful Carozzone, and a young painter named Atilio Franchetti. In the mornings she wrote or painted. Her afternoons were occupied by long solitary walks or hours of reading. Reading and a bent for interior design gave rise to her finest work, *Poe's Room* (1944), which prefigured the *nouveau roman* and much subsequent avantgarde writing, and earned the widow Mendiluce an eminent place in the panorama of Argentinean and Hispanic letters.

This is how she came to write the book. Edelmira read Edgar Allan Poe's essay "Philosophy of Furniture." She was excited. She felt that she had found a soul mate in Poe: their ideas about decoration coincided. She discussed the subject at length with Carozzone and Atilio Franchetti. Following Poe's instructions to the letter, Franchetti painted a picture: an oblong room thirty feet deep and twenty-five feet wide, with a door and two windows in the far wall. He reproduced Poe's furniture, wallpaper and curtains as exactly as possible. Pictorial exactitude, however, was insufficient for Edelmira, so she decided to have a replica of the room built in the garden of her ranch, in accordance with the directions given by Poe. She sent her delegates (antique dealers, cabinet makers, carpenters) hunting for the items described in the essay. The desired but only partly attained result consisted of:

—Large windows reaching down to the floor, set in deep recesses.

—Windowpanes of crimson-tinted glass.

—More than usually massive rosewood framings.

—Inside the recesses, curtains of a thick silver tissue, adapted to the shape of the window and hanging loosely in small volumes.

—Outside the recesses, curtains of an exceedingly rich crimson silk, fringed with a deep network of gold, and lined with the same silver tissue used for the exterior blind.

—The folds of the curtain fabric issuing from beneath a broad entablature of rich giltwork, encircling the room at the junction of the ceiling and walls.

—The drapery thrown open, or closed, by means of a thick rope of gold loosely enveloping it, and resolving itself readily into a knot, no pins or other such devices being apparent.

—The colors of the curtain and their fringe—the tints of crimson and gold—appearing everywhere in profusion, and determining the *character* of the room.

—The carpet—of Saxony material—half an inch think, of the same crimson ground, relieved simply by the appearance of a gold cord (like that festooning the curtains) raised slightly above the surface of the ground, and thrown upon it in such a manner as to form a succession of short irregular curves—one occasionally overlaying the other.

—The walls prepared with a glossy paper of a silver gray tint, spotted with small arabesque devices of a fainter hue of the prevalent crimson.

—Many paintings. Chiefly landscapes of an imaginative cast—such as the fairy grottoes of Stanfield, or Chapman's Lake of the Dismal Swamp—but also three or four female heads, of an ethereal beauty—portraits in the manner of Sully, each picture having a warm but dark tone.

—Not one of the paintings being of small size, since diminutive paintings give that *spotty* look to a room, which is the blemish of so many a fine work of Art overtouched.

—The frames broad but not deep, and richly carved, without being dulled or filigreed.

—The paintings lying flat on the walls, not hanging off with cords.

—One mirror, not very large and nearly circular in shape, hung so that a reflection of a person in any of the ordinary sitting places of the room could not be obtained from it.

—The only seats being two large, low sofas of rosewood and crimson, gold-flowered silk, and two light conversation chairs, also of rosewood.

—A pianoforte made of the same wood, with no cover, and thrown open.

—An octagonal table—also without cover—formed altogether of the richest gold-threaded marble, placed near one of the sofas.

—A profusion of sweet and vivid flowers blooming in four large and gorgeous Sèvres vases, set in each of the slightly rounded angles of the room.

—A tall candelabrum, bearing a small antique lamp with

highly perfumed oil, standing beside one of the sofas (upon which slept Poe's friend, the possessor of this ideal room).

—Some light and graceful hanging shelves, with golden edges and crimson silk cords with gold tassels, sustaining two or three hundred magnificently bound books.

—Beyond these things, no furniture, except for an Argand lamp, with a plain, crimson-tinted ground-glass shade, depending from the lofty vaulted ceiling by a single slender gold chain and throwing a tranquil but magical radiance over all.

The Argand lamp was not particularly difficult to procure. Nor were the curtains, the carpet or the sofas. The wallpaper proved more problematic, but the widow Mendiluce dealt directly with a manufacturer, providing a pattern specially designed by Franchetti. Paintings by Stanfield or Chapman were not to be had, but the painter and his friend Arturo Velasco, himself a promising young artist, produced a number of works, which finally satisfied Edelmira's desires. The rosewood piano also posed a number of problems, all of which were eventually solved.

When the reconstruction of the room was complete, Edelmira judged that the time to write had come. The first part of "Poe's Room" is a detailed description of the same. The second part is a treatise on good taste and interior design, which develops a number of Poe's precepts. The third part is devoted to the building of the room on a lawn in the garden of Edelmira's ranch in Azul. The fourth part is a meticulous account of the search for the furniture. The fifth part is a description of the reconstructed room, similar to but also different from the room conceived by Poe, with a particular emphasis on the light, the color crimson, the origin and state of conservation of various pieces of furniture, the quality of the paintings (every one of which is described, without sparing the reader a single detail). The sixth, final and probably briefest part is a portrait of Poe's friend, the dozing man. Certain perhaps over-ingenious critics identified that figure as the recently deceased Sebastian Mendiluce.

The book made little impact at the time of its publication. On this occasion, however, Edelmira was so sure of what she had written that the general incomprehension hardly affected her.

According to her enemies, during 1945 and 1946 she made frequent visits to deserted beaches and little-known coves, where she welcomed the clandestine travelers arriving in what was left of Admiral Doenitz's submarine fleet. It has also been claimed that she financed the magazine *The Fourth Reich in Argentina* and, subsequently, the publishing house of the same name.

A revised and enlarged edition of *Poe's Room* appeared in 1947. It included a reproduction of Franchetti's painting, showing a view of the room from the doorway. The sleeping man is dimly visible in profile. It could, in fact, be Sebastian Mendiluce. It could also be any heavily built man.

In 1948, while continuing to publish *Modern Argentina*, Edelmira launched a new magazine, *American Letters*, giving her children, Juan and Luz, editorial control. Shortly afterward, she left for Europe, where she would remain until 1955. It has been suggested that an irreconcilable enmity between Edelmira and Eva Peron was the cause of this long exile. Nevertheless, many photographs from the period show the two women together at cocktail and birthday parties, receptions, opening nights, and sporting events. Evita, in all likelihood, could not get beyond page ten of *Poe's Room*, and Edelmira would certainly not have approved of the first lady's social background, but documents and letters written by third parties indicate that they had embarked upon shared projects, such as the creation of a major museum of contemporary Argentinean art (to be designed by Edelmira and the young architect Hugo Bossi), including artist residences, with a full catering service, a feature quite unique among the great museums of the world, the aim being to facilitate the creative work—and daily life—of young and not-so-young exponents of modern painting, and consequently to prevent their emigration to Paris or New York. Some people claim to have seen a film script drafted by the two ladies, about the life and misfortunes of an innocent young Don Juan (to be played by Hugo del Carril), but like so many other things, the draft has been lost.

What we know for certain is that Edelmira did not return to Argentina until 1955, by which time the rising star in literary Buenos Aires was her daughter, Luz Mendiluce.

Edelmira's later years were not prolific. Apart from her *Collected Poems* (the first volume appeared in 1962, the second in 1979), she was to publish only three more books: a volume of memoirs, *The Century as I Have Lived It* (1968), written with the help of the ever-faithful Carozzone; followed by a collection of very short stories, *Churches and Cemeteries of Europe* (1972), distinguished by the author's abundant common sense; and, finally, a gathering of unpublished early poems, *Fervor* (1985).

In her roles as patroness of the arts and promoter of young talent, however, Edelmira remained as active as ever. Countless volumes included a foreword, a preface or an afterword by the widow Mendiluce; she also personally financed the first editions of innumerable works. Of the books for which she wrote prefaces, two deserve a special mention: *Stale Hearts and Young Hearts* by Julián Rico Anaya, a novel which provoked a heated controversy both in Argentina and abroad on its publication in 1978, and *The Invisible Adorers*, by Carola Leyva, a collection of poems intended to put an end to the sterile poetry debate that had been going on in certain Argentinean circles since the *Second Surrealist Manifesto*. Among the books she subsidized, two titles stand out indisputably: *The Kids of Puerto Argentino*, a perhaps somewhat exaggerated memoir of the Falklands War, which catapulted the ex-soldier Jorge Esteban Petrovich to literary prominence, and *The Darts and the Wind*, an anthology of work by young, well-bred poets whose aesthetic objectives included avoiding cacophony, vulgar expressions, and ugly-sounding words, and which, with its preface by Juan Mendiluce, sold unexpectedly well.

Edelmira spent the last three years of her life on her ranch in Azul, either in the Poe room, where she would doze and dream of the past, or out on the broad terrace of the main ranch house, absorbed in a book or contemplating the landscape.

She remained lucid (or "furious," as she liked to say) to the end.

## JUAN MENDILUCE THOMPSON

*Buenos Aires, 1920–Buenos Aires, 1991*

As the second child of Edelmira Thompson, Juan realized at an early age that he could do whatever he liked with his life. He tried his hand at sports (he was a passable tennis player and an appalling race-car driver), patronized the arts (or rather fraternized with bohemians and criminals, until prevented from doing so by his father and his vigorous older brother, whose prohibitions were backed up by threats and occasional violence), and studied law, before turning to literature.

At the age of twenty he published his first novel, *The Egoists*, a tale of mystery and youthful exaltation, set in London, Paris and Buenos Aires. The events are precipitated by an apparently insignificant occurrence: a mild-mannered family man suddenly shouts at his wife, ordering her to take the children and leave the house immediately, or put them in a room and lock the door. He then locks himself in the bathroom. After an hour the woman emerges from the locked room in which she has obediently taken refuge, goes to the bathroom and finds her husband dead, with a razor in his hand and his throat slit. This suicide, which seems at first an open and shut case, is investigated by a Scotland Yard detective with a passion for spiritualism, and by one of the dead man's sons. The investigation takes more than fifteen years and serves as a pretext for introducing a gallery of characters, including a young French neo-royalist and a young German Nazi, who are allowed to discourse at length and seem to serve as the author's mouthpieces.

The novel was a success (by 1943, four editions had sold out in Argentina, and sales were strong in Spain, as well as in Chile, Uruguay and other Latin American countries), but Juan Mendiluce decided to forego literature in favor of politics.

For a time he considered himself to be a Falangist and a follower of José Antonio Primo de Rivera. He was anti-USA and anti-capitalist. Later he became a Peronist and held important government posts at the capital and in the province of Córdoba. His career in public service was impeccable. With the demise of Peronism his political inclinations underwent a further transformation: he turned pro-USA (in fact, the Argentinean Left accused him of publishing twenty-five CIA agents in his magazine—an exaggerated figure, by any reckoning), became a partner in one of the major legal firms in Buenos Aires, and was finally appointed ambassador to Spain. On his return from Madrid he published a novel, *The Argentinean Horseman*, in which he bewailed the spiritual poverty of the contemporary world, the decline of piety and compassion, and the incapacity of the modern novel, particularly in its crude and aimless French manifestations, to understand suffering and so to create characters.

He became known as the Argentinean Cato. He fought with his sister, Luz Mendiluce, over control of the family magazine. Having won the fight, he tried to lead a crusade against the lack of feeling in the contemporary novel. To coincide with the publication of his third novel, *Springtime in Madrid*, he launched a campaign against francophilia, the cult of violence, atheism and foreign ideas. *American Letters* and *Modern Argentina* served as platforms, along with the various Buenos Aires dailies, which were keen to publish, although sometimes flabbergasted by, his denunciations of Cortázar, whom he described as unreal and bloodthirsty, and Borges, whose stories, so he claimed, were "parodies of parodies" and whose lifeless characters were derived from worn-out traditions of English and French literature, clearly in decline, "repeating the same old plots ad nauseam." His attacks took in Bioy Casares, Mujica Lainez, Ernesto Sabato (who, in his eyes, personified the cult of violence and gratuitous aggression), Leopoldo Marechal and others.

He was to publish three more novels: *Youthful Ardor*, a look back to the Argentina of 1940; *Pedrito Saldaña the Patagonian*, a story of adventures in the south, a cross between Stevenson and Conrad; and *Luminous Obscurity*, a novel about order and disorder, justice and injustice, God and the Void.

In 1975, he gave up literature once again in favor of politics. He served the Peronist and military governments with equal loyalty. In 1985, after the death of his elder brother, he took over the running of the family businesses, a task he delegated to his nephews and his son in 1989, in order to work on a novel, which he did not finish. This last work, *Sinking Islands*, was published in a critical edition prepared by Edelmiro Carozzone, the son of his mother's secretary. Fifty pages. Conversations among indistinct characters and chaotic descriptions of an endless welter of rivers and seas.

## Luz Mendiluce Thompson

*Berlin 1928–Buenos Aires 1976*

L uz Mendiluce was a lively pretty child, a pensive plump adolescent, and a hapless alcoholic adult. That said, of all the writers in her family, she was the most talented.

Throughout her life she treasured the famous photo of her baby self in Hitler's arms. Set in a richly worked silver frame, it had pride of place in each of her successive living rooms, along with portraits by Argentinean painters, showing her as a child or a teenager, generally accompanied by her mother. Some of those paintings were very fine works of art, yet had a fire broken out in her house, had there been time to save only one thing, it is conceivable that she would have left them to burn and chosen the photograph, even over her own unpublished manuscripts.

She had various stories for the guests who inquired about

that remarkable snapshot. Sometimes she simply said that the baby was an orphan: the photo had been taken at an orphanage, during one of the visits that politicians frequently make to such institutions in a bid for votes and publicity. On other occasions she explained that it was one of Hitler's nieces, a heroic and unfortunate girl, who had died in combat at the age of seventeen, defending Berlin from the Communist hordes. And sometimes she frankly admitted that it was her: Yes, she had been dandled by the Führer. In dreams, she could still feel his strong arms and his warm breath on the top of her head. She said it had probably been one of the happiest moments of her life. And perhaps she was right.

Her talent bloomed early; she published a first collection of poems when she was still seventeen. By the age of eighteen, with three books to her name, she was living more or less on her own, and had decided to marry the Argentinean poet Julio César Lacouture. The marriage proceeded with the family's blessing, in spite of her fiancé's evident deficiencies. Lacouture was young, refined and stylish, as well as remarkably handsome, but penniless and a mediocre poet. For their honeymoon the couple went to the United States and Mexico, and in Mexico City Luz Mendiluce gave a poetry reading. The problems had already begun. Lacouture was a jealous husband. He took revenge by cheating on his wife. One night in Acapulco, Luz went out to find him. Lacouture was at the house of the novelist Pedro de Medina. During the day, a barbecue had been held there in honor of the Argentinean poetess; by night, the house had been transformed into a brothel, in honor of her husband. Luz found Lacouture with two whores. At first she remained calm. She drank a couple of tequilas in the library with Pedro de Medina and the social-realist poet Augusto Zamora, both of whom tried to calm her down. They talked about Baudelaire, Mallarmé, Claudel and Soviet poetry, Paul Valéry and Sor Juana Inés de la Cruz. Sor Juana was the straw that broke the camel's back; Luz exploded. She grabbed the first thing she could find and returned to the bedroom in search of her husband. Lacouture was attempting to get dressed, in an advanced state of inebriation. The scantily clad whores looked on from a corner of the room. Unable to restrain herself, Luz struck her husband on the head with a bronze sculpture of Pallas Athena. Lacouture had to be hospitalized for fifteen days with a severe concussion. They returned to Argentina together but separated after four months.

The failure of her marriage plunged Luz into despair. She took to drinking in dives and having affairs with some of the most unsavory individuals in Buenos Aires. Her well-known poem "I Was Happy with Hitler," misunderstood by the Right and the Left alike, dates from this period. Her mother tried to send her to Europe, but Luz refused. At the time she weighed more than two hundred pounds (she was only five foot two inches tall) and was drinking a bottle of whisky a day.

In 1953, the year in which Stalin and Dylan Thomas died, she published the collection *Tangos of Buenos Aires*, which, as well as a revised version of "I Was Happy with Hitler," contained some of her finest poems: "Stalin," a chaotic fable set among bottles of vodka and incomprehensible shrieks; "Self Portrait," one of the cruelest poems written in Argentina during the fifties, which is no mean claim; "Luz Mendiluce and Love," in the same vein as her self-portrait, but with doses of irony and black humor, which make it somewhat less grueling; and "Apocalypse at Fifty," a promise to kill herself when she reached that age, which those who knew her regarded as optimistic: given her lifestyle, Luz Mendiluce would be lucky to reach the age of thirty.

Little by little there gathered about her a clique of writers too peculiar for her mother's taste and too radical for her brother. *American Letters* became an essential reference point for Nazis and the embittered, for alcoholics and the sexually or economically marginal. Luz Mendiluce assumed the roles of mother figure and high priestess of a new Argentinean poetry, which a fearful literary community would thenceforth attempt to suppress.

In 1958 she fell in love again. This time the object of her affections was a twenty-five-year-old painter. He was blond, blue-eyed and disarmingly stupid. The relationship lasted until 1960, when the painter went to Paris on a fellowship that Luz had obtained for him, through the good offices of her brother Juan. This new disappointment fuelled the elaboration of another major poem, "Argentinean Painting," in which Luz revisited her often stormy relationships with Argentinean painters in her various capacities—as collector, wife and (from an early age) model.

In 1961, having obtained the annulment of her first marriage, Luz took as her wedded husband the poet Mauricio Cáceres, a regular contributor to *American Letters*, and an exponent of what he himself called the "neo-gaucho" style. Having learned her lesson, this time Luz decided to become a model helpmeet and homemaker: she let her husband take control of *American Letters* (which led to numerous disputes with Juan Mendiluce, who accused Cáceres of appropriating funds), gave up writing and dedicated herself body and soul to her wifely duties. With Cáceres in charge of the magazine, the Nazis, the embittered and the sociopaths unanimously espoused the neo-gaucho style. Success went to Cáceres' head. At one point he came to believe that he could do without Luz and the Mendiluce clan. He attacked Juan and Edelmira when he saw fit. He even allowed himself the pleasure of belittling his wife. New muses soon appeared on the scene: young female converts to the manly cause of neo-gaucho poetry who succeeded in catching the master's eye. Until one day Luz, who had seemed completely unaware of her husband's activities, suddenly exploded once again. The incident was extensively covered in the crime pages and gossip columns of the Buenos Aires newspapers. Cáceres and an editor from *American Letters* ended up in the hospital with bullet wounds. While the editor's injuries were minor, Cáceres was not discharged for a month and a half. Luz did not fare much better. Having shot her husband and her husband's friend, she shut herself in the bathroom and swallowed the contents of the medicine chest. This time, there was nothing for it; she had to leave for Europe.

In 1964, after sojourns in various clinics, Luz surprised her scarce but faithful readers once again with a new a collection entitled *Like a Hurricane*: ten poems, one hundred and twenty pages, with a preface by Susy D'Amato (who could hardly understand a line of Luz's poetry but was one of her few remaining friends), brought out by feminist publishers in Mexico, who would soon come to regret having gambled on a "well-known far-Right activist," although, at the time, they had been unaware of Luz's real allegiances, and the poems themselves were free of political allusions, except for the odd unfortunate metaphor (such as "in my heart I am the last Nazi"), always in the context of personal relationships. The book was republished a year later in Argentina, where it garnered a number of favorable reviews.

In 1967, Luz returned to Buenos Aires, where she was to remain for the rest of her life. An aura of mystery enveloped her. In Paris, Jules Albert Ramis had translated practically all of her poetry. She was accompanied by a young Spanish poet, Pedro Barbero, who acted as her secretary and whom she called Pedrito. This Pedrito, as opposed to her Argentinean husbands and lovers, was helpful, attentive (although perhaps a little uncouth) and above all loyal. Luz took control of *American Letters* once again and set up a new publishing house, The Wounded Eagle. She was soon surrounded by a host of followers who laughed at all her jokes. She weighed two hundred and twenty pounds. Her hair came down to her waist. She rarely washed. Her clothes were old and often ragged.

Luz Mendiluce's emotional life now entered a calmer phase. In other words, she ceased to suffer. She took lovers, drank to excess and was prone to occasional cocaine abuse, but always maintained her spiritual balance. She was severe. Her reviews were feared, and eagerly anticipated by those who were not the targets of her venomous, barbed wit. She entered into bitter, public feuds with certain Argentinean poets (all male and famous), cruelly satirizing their homosexuality (a practice of which she disapproved in public, although many of her friends were gay), their humble social backgrounds, or their Communist convictions. Many women writers in Argentina admired her and read her work, although not all of them would admit to it.

The struggle with her brother Juan over the control of *American Letters* (the magazine in which she had invested so much, and the source of so many disappointments) took on epic proportions. She was defeated, but the young remained loyal. She divided her time between a large apartment in Buenos Aires and a ranch in Paraná, which became an artistic commune over which she could reign unopposed. There, by the river, artists conversed, took siestas, drank and painted, unaffected by the political violence beginning to ravage the rest of the country.

But no one could remain safe from harm. One afternoon, Claudia Saldaña visited the ranch with a friend. She was young, she wrote poetry and she was beautiful. For Luz it was love at first sight. Quickly arranging an introduction, the hostess lavished attention upon her visitor. Claudia Saldaña spent an afternoon and a night at the ranch, returning to Rosario, where she lived, the next morning. Luz recited poems, displayed the French translations of her books and the photo of herself as a baby with Hitler, encouraged the young woman to write, asked to read her poems (Claudia Saldaña said they were no good, she was just a beginner), insisted that her guest keep a little wooden figure she happened to pick up, and finally tried to get her drunk, hoping to make her too ill to leave, but Claudia Saldaña left anyway.

After two days spent in an utter daze, Luz realized that she was in love. She felt like a girl. She got hold of Claudia's telephone number in Rosario and called her. She was almost sober; she could barely control her emotions. She asked if they could meet. Claudia agreed: they could meet in Rosario in three days' time. Luz was beside herself; she wanted to see Claudia that night or the next day at the latest. Claudia stood firm: she had binding, prior engagements. What cannot be cannot be, besides which, it's impossible. Luz accepted her conditions with a joyful resignation. That night she cried and danced and drank until she passed out. No doubt it was the first time that anyone had made her feel that way. True love, she confessed to Pedrito, who agreed with everything she said.

The meeting in Rosario was not as marvelous as Luz had hoped. Claudia clearly and frankly set out the reasons why a closer relationship between them was impossible: she was not a lesbian; there was a significant age difference (Luz being more than twenty-five years older); and, finally, their political convictions were deeply dissimilar if not diametrically opposed. "We are mortal enemies," said Claudia sadly. This affirmation seemed to interest Luz. (Sexual preference was a triviality, she felt, in a case of real love. And age was an illusion. But she was intrigued by the idea of being mortal enemies.) Why? Because I'm a Trotskyite and you're a Fascist shit, said Claudia. Luz ignored the insult and laughed. And there's no way around that? she asked, desperately lovesick. No, there's not, said Claudia. What about poetry? asked Luz. Poetry is pretty irrelevant these days, with what's going on in Argentina. Maybe you're right, Luz admitted, on the verge of tears, but maybe you're wrong. It was a sad farewell. Luz had a sky-blue Alfa Romeo sports car. Easing her rotund physique into the driver's seat was no simple task, but she undertook it bravely, with a smile on her face. Claudia looked on from the doorway of the café where they had met, unmoving. Luz pulled away, with the image of Claudia fixed in the rear-view mirror.

In her position anyone else would have given up, but Luz was not anyone. A torrent of creative activity swept her away. In the past, falling in or out of love had dried up the flow of her writing for long periods. Now she wrote like a mad woman, driven perhaps by a presentiment of what destiny had in store. Every night she called Claudia: they talked, argued, read poems to each other (Claudia's were downright bad but Luz was very careful not to say so). Every night, without fail, she begged: when could they meet again? She made wild plans: they could leave Argentina together, go to Brazil, or Paris. At these suggestions the young poet burst out laughing, but there was nothing cruel in her laughter; if anything, it was tinged with sadness.

Suddenly Luz found the countryside and the artistic commune on the Paraná stifling. She decided to return to Buenos Aires. There she tried to resume her social life, see her friends, go to the movies or the theater. But she couldn't. Nor did she have the courage to visit Claudia in Rosario without her permission. It was then that she wrote one of the strangest poems in Argentinean literature: *My Girl*, 750 lines full of love, regrets and irony. She was still calling Claudia every night.

It is not unreasonable to suppose that a sincere, mutual friendship had developed in the course of all those conversations.

In September 1976, bursting with love, Luz leapt into her Alfa Romeo and sped off to Rosario. She wanted to tell Claudia that she was willing to change, that she was, in fact, already changing. She arrived to find Claudia's parents in a desperate state. A group of strangers had kidnapped the young poet. Luz moved heaven and earth, mobilized her friends, used her connections, then those of her mother, her elder brother and finally Juan's connections too, all in vain. Claudia's friends said the army had taken her. Luz refused to believe anything and waited. Two months later Claudia's body was found in a garbage dump in the north of Rosario. The next day Luz set off for Buenos Aires in her Alfa Romeo. Halfway there she crashed into a gas station. The explosion was considerable.

# ITINERANT HEROES
# OR THE FRAGILITY OF MIRRORS

## Ignacio Zubieta

*Bogotá, 1911–Berlin, 1945*

The only son of one of Bogotá's best families, Ignacio Zubieta was destined for pre-eminence from the start, or so it seemed. A good student and an outstanding sportsman, at the age of thirteen he could write and speak fluent English and French. By virtue of his bearing and manly good looks he stood out wherever he happened to be; he had a pleasant manner and a remarkable knowledge of classical Spanish literature (at the age of seventeen, he published a monograph on Garcilaso de la Vega which was unanimously praised in Colombian literary circles). He was a first-rate horseman, the best polo player of his generation, a superb dancer, always irreproachably dressed (although with a slight tendency to favor sportswear), a confirmed bibliophile, and lively but free of vices; everything about him seemed to foretoken the highest achievements, or at least a life of valuable service to his family and the nation. But chance or the terrible historical circumstances in which he happened (and chose) to live warped his destiny irreparably.

At the age of eighteen he published a book of verse in the style of Góngora, recognized by the critics as a valuable and interesting work, but which could certainly not be said to bring anything new to the Colombian poetry of the time. Zubieta realized this, and six months later left for Europe accompanied by his friend Fernandez-Gómez.

In Spain he frequented the high-society salons, which succumbed to his youth and charm, his intelligence and the aura of tragedy already surrounding his tall, slender figure. It was said (by the gossip columnists of the Bogotá newspapers at the time) that he was on intimate terms with the Duchess of Bahamontes, a rich widow twenty years his senior. That, however, was sheer speculation. His apartment in La Castellana was a meeting place for poets, dramatists and painters. He began, but did not finish, a study of the life and work of the sixteenth-century adventurer Emilio Henríquez, and wrote poems, which few people read, since he made no attempt to publish them. He traveled in Europe and North Africa, and from time to time described his journeys in sharp-eyed vignettes dispatched to Colombian periodicals.

In 1933, impelled, some say, by the imminence of a scandal that never finally came to light, he left Spain, and, after a short stay in Paris, visited Russia and the Scandinavian countries. The land of the Soviets made a contradictory and mysterious impression on him: in his irregular contributions to the Colombian press, he expressed his admiration for Muscovite architecture, the wide open, snow-covered spaces, and the Leningrad Ballet. Either he kept his political opinions to himself or he had none. He described Finland as a toy country. Swedish women struck him as caricatural peasants. The Norwegian fjords, he opined, were still awaiting their great poet (he found Ibsen revolting). Six months later he returned to Paris and took up residence in a comfortable apartment in the Rue des Eaux, where he was joined shortly by his faithful companion Fernández-Gómez, who had been obliged to remain in Copenhagen, recovering from a bout of pneumonia.

The Polo Club and artistic gatherings occupied much of his time in Paris. Zubieta became interested in entomology and attended Professor André Thibault's lectures at the Sorbonne. In 1934 he traveled to Berlin with Fernández-Gomez and a new friend, whom he had, more or less, taken under his wing: the young Philippe Lemercier, a painter who specialized in vertiginous landscapes and "scenes of the end of the world."

Shortly after the outbreak of the civil war in Spain, Zubieta and Fernández-Gomez traveled to Barcelona, then to Madrid, where they stayed for three months, visiting the few friends who had not fled. Then, to the considerable surprise of those who knew them, they went across to the nationalist zone and enlisted as volunteers in Franco's army. Zubieta's military career was meteoric, rich in acts of bravery and medals, though not without a number of lulls. He was promoted from second lieutenant to lieutenant, and then, almost immediately, to captain. He is thought to have participated in the closing of the Mérida pocket, the northern campaign, and the Battle of Teruel. Nevertheless, the end of the war found him in Seville, carrying out more or less administrative duties. The Colombian government unofficially nominated him as cultural attaché in Rome, a post he declined. He took part in the somewhat diminished but still delightful Fiestas del Rocío in 1938 and 1939, riding a spirited white colt. The outbreak of the Second World War caught him by surprise in Mauritania, where he was traveling with Fernández-Gómez. During that voyage the Bogotá press received only two articles from the pen of Zubieta, and neither referred to the specific political and social events that he had the opportunity to witness at close range. In the first article, he described the life of certain Saharan insects. In the second, he discussed Arab horses and compared them to the purebloods bred in Colombia. Not a word about the Spanish Civil War, not a word about the calamity looming over Europe, not a word about literature or himself, although his Colombian friends went on waiting for the great work that Zubieta seemed destined to write.

In 1941, at the request of Dionisio Ridruejo, who was a close friend, Zubieta was one of the first to join the Division of Spanish Volunteers, commonly known as the Blue Division. During his training period in Germany, which he found unspeakably dull, he busied himself with translations of Schiller's verse, aided by the ever-faithful Fernández-Gómez. Their versions were published jointly by the magazines *Living Poetry* in Cartagena and *The Poetic and Literary Beacon* in Seville.

In Russia, he took part in various engagements along the Volchov, as well as the battles of Possad and Krassnij-Bor, where his acts of heroism earned him the Iron Cross. In the summer of 1943 he was back in Paris, alone, Fernández-Gómez having remained in Riga, recovering from his wounds in a military hospital.

In Paris, Zubieta resumed his social life. He traveled to Spain with Lemercier. Some say he saw the Duchess of Bahamontes again. A publisher in Madrid brought out a book of his Schiller translations. He was feted, invited to all the parties, and doted on by high society, but he had changed: unrelieved gravity veiled his expression, as if he could sense the imminence of death.

In October, when the Blue Division was repatriated, Fernández-Gómez returned to Spain and the two friends were reunited in Cadiz. With Lemercier they travelled to Seville, to Madrid, where they gave a reading of Schiller's poems to a large and appreciative audience in a university lecture hall, and then to Paris, where they finally settled.

A few months before D-Day, Zubieta made contact with officers from the Brigade Charlemagne, a French unit of the SS, although his name does not appear in the archives. Enlisted as a captain, he returned to the Russian Front, accompanied by the steadfast Fernández-Gómez. In October 1944, Lemercier received a parcel postmarked in Warsaw, containing papers which were to constitute a part of Ignacio Zubieta's literary legacy.

During the last days of the Third Reich, Zubieta was in Berlin, holding out against the siege with a battalion of die-hard French SS. According to Fernández-Gómez's diary, he was killed in street fighting on April 20, 1945. On the 25th of the same month, Fernández-Gómez entrusted his friend's remaining papers to the diplomats of the Swedish legation along with a case of his own manuscripts, which the Swedes passed on to the Colombian ambassador in Germany in 1948. Zubieta's papers finally reached his relatives, and in 1950 they published an exquisite little book in Bogotá: fifteen poems, with illustrations by Lemercier, who had decided to settle in his friend's beautiful South American homeland. The collection was entitled *Cross of Flowers*. None of the poems was more than thirty lines long. The first was entitled "Cross of Veils," the second "Cross of Flowers" and so on (the second to last was "Cross of Iron" and the last "Cross of Ruins"). Their content, as the titles quite clearly suggest, was autobiographical, but had been subjected to hermetic verbal procedures which rendered the poems obscure and cryptic for a reader attempting to retrace the arc of Zubieta's life or penetrate the mystery that would always surround his exile, his choices and his apparently futile death.

Little is known about the remainder of Zubieta's work. According to some, nothing more remained, or only a few disappointing squibs. For a while there was speculation about a diary totaling more than 500 pages, which Zubieta's mother had burned.

In 1959, a far-Right group in Bogotá published a book entitled *Iron Cross: A Colombian in the Struggle Against Bolshevism* (clearly Zubieta was responsible neither for the title nor the subtitle), having obtained the authorization of Lemercier, but not of Zubieta's family, who took the Frenchman and the publishers to court. The novel, or novella (80 pages long, including five photographs of Zubieta in uniform, one of which shows him smiling coldly in a Paris restaurant, exhibiting the only Iron Cross awarded to a Colombian during the Second World War) is a hymn to friendship among soldiers; it balks at none of the clichés that recur in the voluminous literature on that theme, and was described at the time by a critic as a cross between Sven Hassel and José María Pemán.

## JESÚS FERNÁNDEZ-GÓMEZ

### *Cartagena de Indias, 1910–Berlin, 1945*

Until The Fourth Reich in Argentina published two of his books, more than thirty years after his death, the life and work of Jesús Fernández-Gómez remained entirely obscure. One of those books was *The Fighting Years of an American Falangist in Europe*, a 180-page quasi-autobiographical novel, written in thirty days, while the author was recovering from his war wounds in the Riga military hospital; it recounts his adventures in Spain during the Civil War and in Russia as a volunteer in the Division 250, the famous Spanish Blue Division. The other book is a long poetic text entitled *Cosmogony of the New Order*.

This second volume is composed of three thousand verses, each with a note to indicate where and when it was written: Copenhagen 1933—Zaragoza 1938. A poem of epic aspirations, it tells two stories, constantly juxtaposing them and jumping from one to the other: the story of a Germanic warrior who must slay a dragon, and the story of a South American student who must prove his worth in a hostile milieu. One night the Germanic warrior dreams that he has killed the dragon and that henceforth, in the kingdom it had long tyrannized, a new order shall prevail. The South American student dreams that he must kill someone, and in his dream obeys the order, obtains a gun, and enters the victim's bedroom, in which he finds only "a cascade of mirrors, which blind him forever." The Germanic warrior, reassured by his dream, goes unsuspectingly to the battle in which he is to die. The South American student will spend the rest of his life wandering, blind, through the streets of a cold city, paradoxically comforted by the splendor that caused his blindness.

The first pages of *The Fighting Years of an American Falangist in Europe* relate the author's childhood and adolescence in the city of his birth, Cartagena: the "poor but honest and happy family" in which he grew up, the first books he read, the first poems he wrote. Fernández-Gómez goes on to recount how he met Ignacio Zubieta in a Bogotá brothel; how the two young men became friends; the ambitions they shared; and their desire to see the world and break free of family ties. The second part of the book tells of their early years in Europe: the apartment they shared in Madrid, new friends, their first quarrels (occasionally they came to blows), dirty old women and men, how it was impossible to work in the apartment, the long hours Fernández-Gómez spent holed up in the National Library, and travels that were generally pleasant but occasionally wretched.

Fernández-Gómez marvels at his own youth: he writes of his body, his sexual potency, the length of his member, how well he holds his liquor (although he detests alcohol and only drinks to keep Zubieta company), and his ability to go for days without sleep. He also marvels gratefully at the ease with which he can withdraw into himself at moments of crisis, the solace he finds in the practice of literature, the great work he hopes to write, which will "ennoble him, wash away all his sins, endow his life and his sacrifices with meaning," although he declines to divulge the nature of these "sacrifices." He tries to write about himself and not Zubieta, in spite of the fact that Zubieta's shadow "clings around his neck like an obligatory tie or a lethal bond of loyalty."

He does not expand on political themes. He deems Hitler Europe's providential savior, but says little more about him. Physical proximity to power, however, moves him to tears. The book is full of scenes in which, along with Zubieta, he attends soirées, official functions, medal ceremonies, military parades, church services and dances. The men in positions of authority, almost always generals or prelates, are described in lingering detail, with the tenderness of a mother describing her children.

The Civil War is his moment of truth. Fernández-Gómez throws himself into it with enthusiasm and courage, although he realizes at once, and informs his future readers, that the constant companionship of Zubieta will be no small burden. His evocation of Madrid in 1936—a city where he and Zubieta move like ghosts among ghosts, in search of friends hiding from the Red Terror, and visit Latin American embassies where they are received by demoralized diplomats who can tell them little or nothing—is vivid and striking. It does not take Fernández-Gómez long to adapt to the extraordinary circumstances. Army life, the hardships of battle, the marches and countermarches do not dull his keen fighting spirit. He has time to read and write, to help Zubieta, who is largely dependent on him, to think of the future and make plans for his return to Colombia, plans he will never put into practice.

Almost as soon as the Civil War is over, Fernández-Gómez volunteers for the Blue Division's Russian adventure, along with Zubieta, to whom he is closer than ever. The battle of Possad is recounted realistically, in harrowing, unflinching detail, without a trace of lyricism. The descriptions of bodies destroyed by artillery fire occasionally bring to mind the paintings of Francis Bacon. The final pages evoke the sadness of the Riga Hospital, the solitude of the bedridden warrior, far from his friends, left behind to endure the melancholy Baltic evenings, which he compares unfavorably to the evenings of his distant Cartagena.

Although unedited and unrevised, *The Fighting Years of an American Falangist in Europe* has the power of a work based on extreme experience, as well as containing various colorful observations on lesser-known aspects of Ignacio Zubieta's life, over which we shall pass in discreet silence. Among the numerous grievances addressed to Zubieta by his brother in arms convalescing in Riga we note only one, of a purely literary nature, regarding the authorship of the Schiller translations. In any case, and whatever the truth of that matter, we know that the two friends met again, albeit in the presence of a third party, the painter Lemercier, and that together they resumed the struggle, this time in the controversial Brigade Charlemagne. It is hard to know who led whom into that final adventure.

The last work of Fernández-Gómez to come to public notice (although there is no reason to fear that it is really the *last*) was the erotic novella *The Countess of Bracamonte*, which appeared under the Odin imprint in the Colombian city of Cali in the year 1986. The informed reader will have no trouble identifying the protagonist of this story as the Duchess of Bahamontes, and her two antagonists as the inseparable Zubieta and Fernández-Gómez. The novella is not without humor, which is remarkable, given the place and date of its composition: Paris, 1944. Fernández-Gómez no doubt indulged in a certain amount of embellishment. His Duchess of Bracamonte is 35 years old, not forty-something, the estimated age of the real Duchess. In Fernández-Gómez's novel the two young Colombians (Aguirre and Garmendia) share the noble lady's nights. During the day they sleep or write. The descriptions of Andalucian gardens are meticulous and, in their way, interesting.

# FORERUNNERS AND FIGURES
# OF THE ANTI-ENLIGHTENMENT

## MATEO AGUIRRE BENGOECHEA

*Buenos Aires, 1880–Comodoro Rivadavia, 1940*

Owner of a vast ranch in the province of Chubut, which he ran himself and to which few of his friends were granted access, Mateo Aguirre Bengoechea was a living enigma, oscillating between two poles: bucolic contemplation and titanic activity. He collected pistols and knives, admired Florentine but detested Venetian painting, and had an excellent knowledge of English literature. Although he ordered books regularly from stores in Buenos Aires and Europe, his library never held more than a thousand titles. A confirmed bachelor, he nourished a passion for Wagner, a few French poets (Corbière, Catulle Mendès, Laforgue, Banville) and a few German philosophers (Fichte, August-Wilhelm Schlegel, Friedrich Schlegel, Schelling, Schleirmacher). In the room where he wrote as well as dispatched the business of the ranch, there were many maps and farming implements;

on the walls and shelves, dictionaries and handbooks jostled peaceably with faded photographs of the first Aguirres and bright photographs of his prize animals.

He wrote four well-wrought novels, spaced out over the years (*The Storm and the Youths*, 1911; *The Devil's River*, 1918; *Ana and the Warriors*, 1928; and *The Soul of the Waterfall*, 1936), as well as a brief collection of poems, in which he complained that he had been born too soon, in a country that was too young.

He wrote a great many detailed letters to literary figures of all persuasions in America and Europe, whose works he read attentively, although the tone of the correspondence always remained formal.

He detested Alfonso Reyes with a tenacity worthy of a nobler enterprise.

Shortly before his death, in a letter to a friend in Buenos Aires, he foresaw a radiant epoch for the human race, the triumphant dawn of a new golden age, and he wondered whether the Argentinean people would rise to the occasion.

# Silvio Salvático

*Buenos Aires, 1901–Buenos Aires, 1994*

As a young man Salvático advocated, among other things, the re-establishment of the Inquisition; corporal punishment in public; a permanent war against the Chileans, the Paraguayans, or the Bolivians as a kind of gymnastics for the nation; polygamy; the extermination of the Indians to prevent further contamination of the Argentinean race; curtailing the rights of any citizen with Jewish blood; a massive influx of migrants from the Scandinavian countries in order to effect a progressive lightening of the national skin color, darkened by years of promiscuity with the indigenous population; life-long writer's grants; the abolition of tax on artists' incomes; the creation of the largest air force in South America; the colonization of Antarctica; and the building of new cities in Patagonia.

He was a soccer player and a Futurist.

From 1920 to 1929, in addition to frequenting the literary salons and fashionable cafes, he wrote and published more than twelve collections of poems, some of which won municipal and provincial prizes. From 1930 on, burdened by a disastrous marriage and numerous offspring, he worked as a gossip columnist and copy-editor for various newspapers in the capital, hung out in dives, and practised the art of the novel, which stubbornly declined to yield its secrets to him. Three titles resulted: *Fields of Honor* (1936), about semi-secret challenges and duels in a spectral Buenos Aires; *The French Lady* (1949), a story of prostitutes with hearts of gold, tango singers and detectives; and *The Eyes of the Assassin* (1962), a curious precursor to the psycho-killer movies of the seventies and eighties.

He died in an old-age home in Villa Luro, his worldly possessions consisting of a single suitcase full of books and unpublished manuscripts.

His books were never republished. His manuscripts were probably thrown out with the trash or burned by the orderlies.

## Luiz Fontaine Da Souza

*Río de Janeiro, 1900—Río de Janeiro, 1977*

A precocious author, whose *Refutation of Voltaire* (1921) was hailed by Catholic literary circles in Brazil and admired by the academic community on account of its sheer bulk (it was 640 pages long), its critical and bibliographical apparatus, and the author's evident youth. In 1925, as if to fulfill the hopes generated by his first book, Fontaine da Souza published *A Refutation of Diderot* (530 pages), followed two years later by *A Refutation of D'Alembert* (590 pages), thus establishing himself as the country's leading Catholic philosopher.

In 1930, *A Refutation of Montesquieu* (620 pages) appeared, and in 1932 *A Refutation of Rousseau* (605 pages).

In 1935 he spent four months at a clinic for the mentally ill in Petropolis.

In 1937 *The Jewish Question in Europe Followed by a*

*Memorandum on the Brazilian Question* came out: a characteristically capacious book (552 pages), in which Fontaine explained the threats that widespread miscegenation would pose to Brazilian society (disorder, promiscuity, criminality).

The year 1938 saw the publication of *A Refutation of Hegel Followed by a Brief Refutation of Marx and Feuerbach* (635 pages), which many philosophers and even a few general readers considered the work of a lunatic. Fontaine was, irrefutably, well versed in French philosophy (his command of the language was excellent), but not, by any means, in the work of the German philosophers. His "refutation" of Hegel, whom he confuses with Kant on several occasions, and, worse still, with Jean Paul, Hölderlin and Ludwig Tieck, is, according to the critics, a sorry affair.

In 1939, he surprised everyone by publishing a sentimental novella. In a mere 108 pages (another surprise), the book tells how a professor of Portuguese literature set about wooing a rich, young and almost illiterate woman from Novo Hamburgo. Entitled *The Conflict of Opposites*, it sold very few copies, but its delicate style, its intellectual acuity, and the perfect economy of its construction were not lost on certain critics, who praised the book unreservedly.

In 1940, Fontaine was interned again in the Petropolis clinic, where he would remain for three years. During that long stay, broken by Christmas holidays and vacations with his family (always under the strict supervision of a nurse), he wrote a sequel to *The Conflict of Opposites* called *Evening in Porto Alegre*, whose subtitle (*Apocalypse in Novo Hamburgo*) sheds light retrospectively on his work as a whole. The story takes up where *The Conflict of Opposites* left off. Roughly written, with none of the previous volume's delicacy, acuity or economy, *Evening in Porto Alegre* adopts various points of view without changing the narrative voice, which is that of the professor of Portuguese literature, who recounts an interminable yet hectic evening in the southern Brazilian city of Porto Alegre, while simultaneously in Novo Hamburgo (hence the subtitle) servants, family members and later the police are confronted with the body of a rich, illiterate heiress, found in her bedroom, *under* the large canopied bed, with multiple stab wounds. The novel remained unpublished until well into the sixties, for family reasons.

A long silence ensued. In 1943, Fontaine published an article in a Rio newspaper, protesting Brazil's entry into the Second World War. In 1948 he contributed an article to a magazine called *Brazilian Woman* on the flowers and legends of Pará, especially the region between the rivers Tapajoz and Xingu.

And that was all until 1955 and the publication of his *Critique of Sartre's Being and Nothingness, Volume I* (350 pages), which deals only with sections two and three of Sartre's introduction, "In Pursuit of Being": "The Phenomenon of Being and the Being of the Phenomenon" and "The Prereflective Cogito and the Being of the *Percipere*." In his denigration, Fontaine ranges from the pre-Socratic philosophers to the movies of Chaplin and Buster Keaton. Volume II (320 pages) appeared in 1957, dealing with the fifth and sixth sections of the introduction to Sartre's work, "The Ontological Proof" and "Being-in-Itself." It would be an exaggeration to say that either book sent so much as a ripple through philosophical and academic circles in Brazil.

In 1960, the third volume appeared. In exactly 600 pages it broaches the third, fourth and fifth sections ("The Dialectical Concept of Nothingness," "The Phenomenological Concept of Nothingness" and "The Origin of Nothingness") of the first chapter ("The Origin of Negation") in Part I ("The Problem of Nothingness") and the first, second and third sections ("Bad Faith and Falsehood," "Patterns of Bad Faith," "The 'Faith' of Bad Faith") of the second chapter ("Bad Faith").

In 1961, a sepulchral silence, which Fontaine's publisher made no effort to break, greeted the publication of the fourth volume (555 pages), which tackles the five sections ("Presence to Self," "The Facticity of the For-Itself," "The For-Itself and the Being of Value," "The For-Itself and the Being of Possibilities," "The Self and the Circuit of Selfness") of the first chapter ("Immediate Structures of the For-Itself") of Part II ("Being-for-Itself") and the second and third sections ("The Ontology of Temporality" and "Original Temporality and Psychic Temporality: Reflection") of the second chapter ("Temporality").

In 1962, the fifth volume (720 pages) appeared, in which, passing over the third chapter ("Transcendence") of Part II, almost all the sections of the first chapter ("The Existence of Others") of Part III ("Being-for-Others"), and the whole of the second chapter ("The Body"), Fontaine makes a wild and reckless leap to the third section ("Husserl, Hegel, Heidegger") of the first chapter and the three sections ("First Attitude Toward Others: Love, Language, Masochism," "Second Attitude Toward Others: Indifference, Desire, Hate, Sadism" and "'Being-With' (*Mitsein*) and the 'We'") of the third chapter ("Concrete Relations with Others") of Part III.

In 1963, while he was working on the sixth volume, his siblings and nephews were obliged to have him interned once again in the clinic, where he remained until 1970. He never resumed his writing. Death took him by surprise seven years later in his comfortable apartment in the Leblon neighborhood of Rio, as he listened to a record by the Argentinean composer Tito Vásquez, and looked out of the window at night falling over the city, passing cars, people chatting on the sidewalks, lights coming on and going out, and windows being closed.

# ERNESTO PÉREZ MASÓN

*Matanzas, 1908–New York, 1980*

The reputation of Ernesto Pérez Masón, realist, naturalist and expressionist novelist, exponent of the decadent style and social realism, rests on a series of twenty works, beginning with the splendid story "Heartless" (Havana, 1930), a nightmare with Kafkaesque echoes, written at a time when the work of Kafka was little known in the Caribbean, and ending with the abrasive, caustic, embittered prose of *Don Juan in Havana* (Miami, 1979).

A rather atypical member of the group that formed around the magazine *Orígenes*, he maintained a legendary feud with Lezama Lima. On three occasions, he challenged the author of *Paradiso* to a duel. The first time, in 1945, the affair was to be decided, so he declared, on the little field he owned outside Pinar del Río, which had inspired him to write numerous pages about the deep joy of land ownership, a condition he had come to see as the ontological equivalent of destiny. Naturally Lezama spurned his challenge.

On the second occasion, in 1954, the site chosen for the duel, to be fought with sabers, was the patio of a brothel in Havana. Once again, Lezama failed to appear.

The third and final challenge took place in 1963; the designated field of honor was the back garden of a house belonging to Dr. Antonio Nualart, in which a party attended by painters and poets was under way, and it was to be a fist fight, in the traditional Cuban manner. Lezama, who by pure chance happened to be at the party, managed to slip away again, with the help of Eliseo Diego and Cintio Vitier. But this time Pérez Masón's show of bravado landed him in trouble. Half an hour later the police arrived and, after a short discussion, arrested him. The situation degenerated at the police station. According to the police, Pérez Masón hit an officer in the eye. According to Pérez Masón, the whole thing was an ambush cleverly contrived by Lezama and Castro's regime, in an unholy alliance forged with the express purpose of destroying him. The upshot of the incident was a fifteen-day prison term.

That was not to be Pérez Masón's last visit to the jails of socialist Cuba. In 1965 he published *Poor Man's Soup*, which related—in an irreproachable style, worthy of Sholokov—the hardships of a large family living in Havana in 1950. The novel comprised fourteen chapters. The first began: "Lucia was a black woman from . . ."; the second: "Only after serving her father . . ."; the third: "Nothing had come easily to Juan . . ."; the fourth: "Gradually, tenderly, she drew him towards her . . ." The censor quickly smelled a rat. The first letters of each chapter made up the acrostic LONG LIVE

HITLER. A major scandal broke out. Pérez Masón defended himself haughtily: it was a simple coincidence. The censors set to work in earnest, and made a fresh discovery: the first letters of each chapter's second paragraph made up another acrostic—THIS PLACE SUCKS. And those of the third paragraph spelled: USA WHERE ARE YOU. And the fourth paragraph: KISS MY CUBAN ASS. And so, since each chapter, without exception, contained twenty-five paragraphs, the censors and the general public soon discovered twenty-five acrostics. I screwed up, Pérez Masón would say later: They were too obvious, but if I'd made it much harder, no one would have realized.

In the end, he was sentenced to three years in prison, but served only two, during which his early novels came out in English and French. They include *The Witches*, a misogynistic book full of stories opening onto other stories, which in turn open onto yet others, and whose structure or lack of structure recalls certain works of Raymond Roussel; *The Enterprise of the Masons*, a paradigmatic and paradoxical work, saluted on its publication in 1940 by Virgilio Piñera (who saw it as a Cuban version of *Gargantua and Pantagruel),* in which it is never entirely clear whether Pérez Masón is talking about the business acumen of his ancestors or about the members of a Masonic lodge who met at the end of the nineteenth century in a sugar refinery to plan the Cuban Revolution and the worldwide revolution to follow; and *The Gallows Tree* (1946), written in a dark, Caribbean Gothic vein, unprecedented at the time, in which the author reveals his hatred of Communists (although, oddly, he devotes a whole chapter, the third, to the military fortunes and misfortunes of Marshall Zhukov, the hero of Moscow, Stalingrad and Berlin, and that chapter, taken on its own—it has in fact little to do with the rest of the book—is one of the strangest and most brilliant passages in Latin American literature between 1900 and 1950), as well as his hatred of homosexuals, Jews and blacks, thus earning the enmity of Virgilio Piñera, who always admitted, nevertheless, that the novel, arguably the author's best, had a disquieting power, like a sleeping crocodile.

Until the triumph of the revolution, that is, for almost all of his working life, Pérez Masón taught graduate-level French literature classes. During the fifties he tried unsuccessfully to cultivate peanuts and yams in his inspiring little field near Pinar del Río, which was eventually expropriated by the new authorities. There are endless stories in circulation about his life in Havana after getting out of jail, most of them pure fiction. He is said to have been a police informer, to have written speeches and tirades for one of the regime's well-known political figures, founded a secret society of fascist poets and assassins, practiced Afro-Cuban rituals, and visited all the island's writers, painters and musicians, asking them to plead his cause with the authorities. All I want is to work, he said, just work and live doing the only thing I know how to do. That is, writing.

At the time of his release from prison he had finished a 200-page novel, which no Cuban publisher dared to take on. The action took place in the sixties, during the early years of the literacy campaign. It was an impeccably accomplished book, and the censors sifted its pages searching for encrypted messages, but in vain. Even so, it was unpublishable, and Pérez Masón finally burned the only three manuscript copies. Years later, in his memoirs, he would claim that the whole novel, from the first to the last page, was a handbook of cryptography, a "Super Enigma," although of course he no longer had the text to prove it, and the exiled Cubans of Miami, who had not forgotten his early and somewhat hasty hagiographies of Fidel and Raúl Castro, Camilo Cienfuegos and Che Guevara, received his assertion with indifference, if not disbelief. Pérez Masón answered them by publishing a curious novella under the pseudonym Abelard of Rotterdam: an erotic and fiercely anti-USA fantasy, whose protagonists were General Eisenhower and General Patton.

In 1970, or so Pérez Masón claims in his memoirs, he managed to found a group called Artists and Writers of the Counterrevolution. The group consisted of the painter Alcides Urrutia and the poet Juan José Lasa Mardones, two entirely mysterious individuals, probably invented by Pérez Masón himself, unless they were pseudonyms used by never-identified pro-Castro writers who at some point went crazy or decided to play a double game. According to some critics, the acronym AWC secretly stood for the Aryan Writers of Cuba. In any case the Artists and Writers of the Counterrevolution or the Aryan Writers of Cuba (or the Caribbean?) remained entirely unknown until Pérez Masón, who by that stage was comfortably settled in New York, published his memoirs.

The years of his ostracism are shrouded in legend. Perhaps he was jailed again, perhaps not.

But in 1975, after many failed attempts, he managed to get out of Cuba and settle in New York, where he devoted his time and energy—working more than ten hours a day—to writing and polemics. He died five years later. Surprisingly, his name figures in the *Dictionary of Cuban Authors* (Havana, 1978), which omits Guillermo Cabrera Infante.

*POÈTES MAUDITS*

PEDRO GONZÁLEZ CARRERA

*Concepción, 1920–Valdivia, 1961*

A few hagiographies of Pedro González Carrera have come down to us; all concur in affirming, and perhaps with good reason, that his work was as brilliant as his life was dull. He came from a humble background, worked as a grammar school teacher, got married at twenty and fathered seven children; his life was a series of moves from post to post—always in small towns or mountain villages—and economic hardships, seasoned with family tragedies and personal affronts.

His first poems were adolescent imitations of Campoamor, Espronceda and the Spanish Romantics. At the age of twenty-one, he was published for the first time in *Southern Flowers*, a magazine devoted to "agriculture, stockbreeding, education and fishing," edited at the time by a group of grammar school teachers from Concepción and Talcahuano, whose leading light was Florencio Capó, a friend of the poet since childhood. At twenty-four, according to his biographers, González tried to get a second poem published, this time in the *Journal of the Pedagogical Institute of Santiago*. Capó, who by then had moved to the capital and was among the journal's contributors, submitted the poem, as he would later say, sight unseen, and it was published along with twenty other texts by as many poets, who were teachers in Santiago or, for the most part, in the provinces, and who made up the core of the magazine's readership. The scandal was immediate and momentous, albeit limited to Chile's teaching community.

The poem was a far, far cry from the blandishments of Campoamor; in thirty precise and limpid verses, it vindicated Il Duce's vilified armies and the derided courage of the Italians (who, at the time, in both pro-Allied and pro-German circles, were assumed to be a race of cowards; for instance, in relation to a possible border conflict with the Italianized Argentineans, a Santiago politician had famously remarked that with a company of good Chilean border guards the government could halt and rout a division of invading wops), while also, and here lay its originality, denying Italy's flagrant defeat, and promising an ultimate victory, to be achieved "by novel, unexpected, marvelous means."

As a result of the furor—of which González, teaching at the time in a remote village somewhere near Santa Bárbara, was informed by three letters, in one of which Capó disapproved of González's position, reaffirmed his friendship and washed his hands of the whole matter—the magazine *Iron Heart* attempted to contact the poet, and the Ministry of Education added his name to a long and futile list of possible Fascist fifth columnists.

His next venture into print dates from 1947. It consists of three poems which blend lyric and narrative impulses, as well as modernist and surrealist metaphors, employing images that are, at times, disconcerting: González sees men in armor, "Merovingians from another planet," walking down endless wooden corridors; he sees blond women sleeping in the open beside putrid streams; he sees machines whose functions he dimly intuits as they move through dark nights, their headlights shining "like diadems of canine teeth." He sees, but does not describe, acts that frighten him, but to which he feels irresistibly drawn. The action unfolds not in this world but in a parallel universe where "Will and Fear are one and the same."

The following year, he published another three poems in *Iron Heart*, which by then had moved its editorial operations to Punta Arenas. These poems revisit the same scenes and recreate the same atmospheres as the previous three, with slight variations. In a letter to his friend Capó, dated March 8, 1947, along with the usual complaints about his job and tales of familial woe, González reveals that his poetic illumination took place in the summer of 1943, during which he was visited for the first time by the extraterrestrial Merovingians. But did they visit him in a dream or in reality? On that point González remains unclear. In the letter to Capó, he reflects at length on glossolalia, epiphanies and the miraculous images that appear at the ends of tunnels. He explains how, having worked until nightfall in his little country school, feeling very sleepy and hungry, he tried to get up and go home. Unsuccessfully, at least in part, as far as one can tell from his account. An hour later he woke up in a nearby field, lying on the ground, face up, under an exceptionally starry night sky, with all of the poems, from the first word to the last, in his head. Having read the copy of *Iron Heart* sent by González along with his letter, Capó advised his friend to make an urgent request for a transfer, or else the solitude would end up driving him crazy.

González took his advice about the transfer but stubbornly continued to exploit his peculiar poetic vein. The next three poems he published (not in *Iron Heart*, which had folded, but in the cultural supplement of a Santiago newspaper) are free of surrealist images, symbolist baggage and modernist vagaries (González, it must be said, knew almost nothing of the three schools in question). His verse has become concise, his images simple; the figures that recurred in the six previous poems have also undergone a transformation: the Merovingian warriors have become robots, the women are now dying beside putrid streams of consciousness, and the mysterious tractors plowing the fields without rhyme or reason are either secret vessels sent from Antarctica, or Miracles (with a capital letter). And now these figures are counterbalanced by a sketchy presence, that of the author himself, adrift in the vast spaces of the fatherland, observing the apparitions like a registrar of marvels, but unenlightened finally as to their causes, phenomenology or ultimate purpose.

In 1955, at the cost of great personal sacrifice and tremendous effort, González financed the publication of a chapbook containing twelve poems, printed by a press in Cauquenes, capital of the province of Maul, where he had been transferred. The little book was entitled *Twelve*, and the cover, which was the author's own work, is noteworthy in its own right, as it was the first of many drawings he produced to accompany his poems (the others came to light only after his death). The letters of the word *Twelve* on the cover, equipped with eagle talons, grip a swastika in flames, beneath which there seems to be a sea with waves, drawn in a childlike style. And under the sea, between the waves, a child can in fact be glimpsed, crying, "Mom, I'm scared!" The speech bubble is blurred. Under the child and the sea are lines and blotches, which might be volcanoes or printing defects.

The twelve new poems add new figures and landscapes to the repertoire developed in the previous nine. The robots, the streams of consciousness and the ships are supplemented with Destiny and Will, personified by two stowaways in the holds of a ship, as well as The Disease Machine, The Language Machine, The Memory Machine (which has been damaged since the beginning of time), The Potentiality Machine and The Precision Machine. The only human figure in the earlier poems (that of González himself) is joined by the Advocate of Cruelty, a strange character who sometimes speaks like a regular Chilean guy (or rather, like a grammar school teacher's *idea* of a regular guy) and sometimes like a sibyl or a Greek soothsayer. The setting is the same as for the earlier poems: an open field in the middle of the night, or a theater of colossal dimensions situated in the heart of Chile.

González sent the chapbook to various newspapers in Santiago and the provinces, but in spite of his best efforts, it made almost no impression. A gossip columnist in Valparaiso wrote a humorous review entitled "Our Rural Jules Verne." A left-wing paper cited González, along with many others, as an example of the growing Fascist influence on the nation's cultural life. But in fact no one, on the Right or the Left, was reading his poems, much less supporting him, except perhaps Florencio Capó, who lived far away, and whose friendship had been sorely tried by the cover of *Twelve*. In Cauquenes, two stationery stores displayed the book for a month. Then they returned the copies to the author.

Stubbornly, González went on writing and drawing. In 1959 he sent the manuscript of a novel to two publishers in Santiago. Both rejected it. In a letter to Capó he refers to the novel as his scientific work, a compendium of his scientific knowledge, which he will bequeath to posterity, although it was no secret that he knew next to nothing about physics, astrophysics, chemistry, biology or astronomy. When he was transferred to a village near Valdivia, his health, which had been delicate at the best of times, deteriorated sharply. In June 1961, he died in the Valdivia Provincial Hospital at the age of forty. He was buried in a common grave.

Many years later, thanks to the efforts of Ezequiel Arancibia and Juan Herring Lazo, who had read González's contribution to *Iron Heart*, scholarly research into the poet's work began in earnest. Luckily, most of his papers had been kept, first by his widow, then by one of his daughters. And in 1976, Florencio Capó entrusted the scholars with the letters he had received from his old friend.

The first volume of the *Complete Poems* (350 pages), edited and annotated by Arancibia, appeared in 1975.

The second and final volume (480 pages) followed in 1977. It included González's overall plan for his works, sketched out in note form back in 1945, and a great many drawings, which were highly original in a number of respects, and whose function was to help the author himself to understand, as he put it, the "avalanche of novel revelations troubling my soul."

In 1980, *The Advocate of Cruelty* was published, with the strange dedication: "To my Italian friend, the unknown soldier, the laughing victim." The novel is 150 pages long, and elicits a certain wariness on the part of the reader. It makes no concessions to fashion (although exiled as he was in Maule, González can hardly have been aware of the literary fashions of his day), or to the reader, or to the author himself. Cold, but spellbound and spellbinding, as Arancibia writes in his preface.

In 1982, a slim, ninety-page volume containing his entire correspondence concluded the series of posthumous publications. It contains the letters he wrote to his fiancée, to his friend Capó (which account for the greater part of the book), to magazine editors, colleagues, and officials in the Ministry of Education. The letters reveal little about his work, but a great deal about the suffering he had to endure.

Today, thanks to the enterprising promoters and editors of the *Southern Hemisphere Review*, two streets bear the name of Pedro González Carrera, one in a far-flung suburb of Cauquenes, the other near a treeless square in the northern part of Valvidia. Few people know whom they commemorate.

ANDRÉS CEPEDA CEPEDA
known as *The Page*


*Arequipa, 1940–Arequipa, 1986*


The first literary ventures of Andrés Cepeda Cepeda were marked by the beneficent influence of Marcos Ricardo Alarcón Chamiso, a local poet and musician with whom he used to spend afternoons jointly composing poems in a restaurant called La Góndola Andina, in his hometown of Arequipa. In 1960 he published a slim volume entitled *The Destiny of Pizarro Street*, whose subtitle, *The Infinite Doors*, suggests a series of Pizarro Streets, scattered throughout the continent, which, once discovered (although as a rule they remain hidden) have the power to provide a new framework for *American perception*, in which *will* and *dream* shall blend in a new vision of reality—an *American awakening*. The thirteen poems of *The Destiny of Pizarro Street*, composed in rather uncertain hendecasyllabics, failed to attract critical attention: only Alarcón Chamiso reviewed the book, in the *Arequipa Herald*, praising its musicality above all, the "syllabic mystery that lurks behind the fiery style" of the author.

In 1962, Cepeda began to contribute to the bimonthly magazine *Panorama,* edited in Lima by the controversial lawyer Antonio Sánchez Luján. The two men met when Sánchez Luján came to Arequipa to be the guest of honor at a Rotary Club dinner. As a result, The Page was born; henceforth Cepeda used that pseudonym to sign articles ranging from political diatribes to movie and book reviews. In 1965 he combined his work for *Panorama* with a daily column in the *Peruvian Evening News*, which belonged to Pedro Argote, the flour and seafood magnate, an old friend of Sánchez Luján. There Andrés Cepeda enjoyed his few moments of glory: his articles, ranging widely, like those of Dr. Johnson, provoked hostility and lasting resentment. He gave his opinion on any topic, and believed he had a solution for everything. He made errors of judgment, was sued along with the paper, and, one by one, lost every case. In 1968, while leading a whirlwind life in Lima, he republished *The Destiny of Pizarro Street*, supplementing the original thirteen poems with five new ones, the elaboration of which, he confessed in his column ("A Poet's Work"), had cost him eight years of intense effort. This time, because of The Page's notoriety, the critics did not ignore the book but fell upon it, each trying to outdo the savagery of his peers. Among the expressions employed were the following: prehistoric Nazi, moron, champion of the bourgeoisie, puppet of capitalism, CIA agent, poetaster intent on debasing public taste, plagiarist (he was accused of copying Eguren, Salazar Bondy, and Saint-John Perse, in the last case by a very young poet from San Marcos, whose ac-

cusation sparked another polemic opposing academic followers and detractors of Saint-John Perse), gutter thug, cut-rate
prophet, rapist of the Spanish language, satanically inspired
versifier, product of a provincial education, upstart, delirious
half-blood, etc., etc.

The differences between the first and second editions of
*The Destiny of Pizarro Street* are not especially striking. Some,
nevertheless, are worthy of note. The most obvious difference
is that the Arequipa edition is made up of thirteen poems
and is dedicated to Cepeda's mentor, Alarcón Chamiso, while
the Lima edition contains eighteen poems but no dedication.
Of the original thirteen poems, only the eighth, the twelfth
and the thirteenth have been revised, and the changes are
slight—simple word-substitutions (*impasse* instead of *difficulty*, *judgment* instead of *talent*, *miscellaneous* instead of
*various*)—which do not greatly alter the original meaning. As
to the five new poems, they seem to be cut from the same
cloth: hendecasyllabics, a supposedly vigorous tone, an overall
aim that remains rather vague, regular versification with occasional shoe-horning, and nothing in the least bit original.
And yet the addition of these five poems changes the meaning
or deepens and illuminates the interpretation of the first thirteen. What seemed a welter of mystery, murkiness and hack-
neyed allusions to mythical figures resolves into clarity and
method, explicit commitments and proposals. And what does
The Page propose? To what is he committed? A return to the
Iron Age, which for him coincides roughly with the life and
times of Pizarro. Inter-racial conflict in Peru (although when
he says Peru, and this is perhaps more important than his
theory of racial struggle, to which he devotes no more than
a couplet, he is also including Chile, Bolivia and Ecuador).

The ensuing conflict between Peru and Argentina (including Uruguay and Paraguay), which he dubs "the Combat of Castor and Pollux." The uncertain victory. The possible defeat of both sides, which he prophesies for the thirty-third year of the third millennium. In the final three lines, he alludes laboriously to the birth of a blond child in the ruins of a sepulchral Lima.

Cepeda's notoriety as a poet lasted no more than a month. The Page's career continued for some time, although his glory days were over. Losing the libel cases was a rude awakening; then he was sacked by the *Peruvian Evening News*, which offered him up as a propitiatory victim to placate both a beer magnate of indigenous origins and the secretary of a certain ministry whom Cepeda had publicly taken to task for his ineptitude (which was widely acknowledged and admitted).

He did not publish any more books.

In his final years he relied on *Panorama* and stints of radio journalism. He also worked occasionally as a copy-editor. Initially he was surrounded by a small group of admirers, known as The Pages, but gradually time dispersed them. In 1982, he returned to Arequipa, where he set up a small fruit store. He died of a stroke in the spring of 1986.

WANDERING WOMEN
OF LETTERS

# Irma Carrasco

*Puebla, Mexico, 1910–Mexico City, 1966*

A Mexican poet inclined to mysticism and tormented phraseology. At the age of twenty she published her first collection of verse, *The Voice You Withered*, which bears witness to a stubborn and sometimes fanatical reading of Sor Juana Inez de la Cruz.

Her grandparents and parents were supporters of Porfírio Díaz. Her elder brother was a priest who embraced the cause of the Cristeros and was executed by firing squad in 1928. In her 1933 collection, *The Destiny of Women*, she confessed that she was in love with God, Life and a New Mexican Dawn, to which she also referred indiscriminately as *resurrection, awakening, dreaming, falling in love, forgiveness* and *marriage*.

Being open-minded, she frequented the salons of Mexican high society as well as the haunts of the avant-garde, where her charm and frankness immediately won over the revolutionary painters and writers, who welcomed her warmly although they were well aware of her conservative ideas.

In 1934 she published *The Paradox of the Cloud*, fifteen sonnets in the style of Góngora, and *A Tableau of Volcanoes*, a series of highly personal poems, specimens of Catholic feminism *avant la lettre*. She was boundlessly prolific. Her optimism was contagious. Her personality was delightful. She radiated beauty and serenity.

In 1935, after a five-month engagement, which at the time was considered too short, she married Gabino Barreda, an architect from Hermosillo, Sonora, who was also a semi-covert Stalinist and a notorious Don Juan. They spent their honeymoon in the Sonora desert, where both husband and wife found the lonely expanses inspiring.

On their return, they moved into a colonial house in Coyoacán, which, thanks to Barreda, became the first colonial house with steel and glass walls. Outwardly they made an enviable couple: both were young; they were not short of money; Barreda was the prototype of the brilliant, idealistic architect, with grand plans for the new cities of the continent; while Irma was the prototype of the beautiful, upper-class woman, self-assured and proud, but also intelligent and serene, endowed with the ballast of good sense required to keep a marriage of artists on an even keel.

Real life, however, was a different matter, and for Irma it was not without disappointments. Barreda cheated on her with common chorus girls. He had no time for niceties and beat her almost every day. He used to put her down in public, and held her family in contempt, referring to them, in conversations with friends and strangers, as "a bunch of Cristero assholes . . . good for nothing except target practice." Real life can sometimes bear an unsettling resemblance to nightmares.

In 1937 the couple traveled to Spain. Barreda went to save the Republic, Irma to save her marriage. In Madrid, while Franco's air support bombed the city, in room 304 of the Hotel Splendor, Irma was subjected to the most brutal beating of her life.

The next day, without a word to her husband, she left the Spanish capital, bound for Paris. A week later Barreda set off in search of her, but Irma had already left Paris, and gone back across the Spanish border to Burgos, in the nationalist zone, where she was welcomed by the mother superior of a discalced Carmelite convent, to whom she was distantly related.

The life she led for the rest of the war is legendary. According to various reports she worked as a nurse in first aid stations on the front lines, wrote and acted in *tableaux vivants* to raise the soldiers' morale, and befriended the Colombian Catholic poets Ignacio Zubieta and Jesús Fernández-Gómez. General Muñoz Grande is said to have cried on seeing her for the first time, because he knew she would never be his. She was, it seems, affectionately known to the young Falangist poets as *Guadalupe* or *The Angel of the Trenches*.

In 1939, a pamphlet entitled *The Triumph of Virtue or The Triumph of God* was printed in Salamanca, containing five or her poems, celebrating Franco's victory in finely wrought, symmetrically balanced lines. In 1940, having moved to Madrid, she published another book of poetry, *Spain's Gift*, and a play, *A Tranquil Night in Burgos*, which was soon successfully staged and later adapted for the screen (it explores the joyous vacillation of a novice about to take the veil). In 1941, she traveled around Europe with a group of Spanish artists on a triumphant promotional tour sponsored by the German Ministry of Culture. She visited Rome and Greece, Hungary and Rumania (where she visited the house of General Entrescu, and met his fiancée, the Argentinean poet Daniela de Montecristo, to whom she took an immediate dislike: "Everything about her suggests that this woman is a wh—," she wrote in her diary); she traveled by boat on the Rhine and the Danube. Her talent, previously dulled by insufficient stimulation and by a lack or an excess of love, emerged and shone again in all its splendor. This rebirth nurtured the seeds of a new and fervent vocation: journalism. She wrote articles, portraits of political and military figures, described the cities she visited in vivid and picturesque detail, attended to Paris fashions and to the problems and concerns of the Roman Curia. Magazines and newspapers in Mexico, Argentina, Bolivia and Paraguay published her features and stories.

In 1942, Mexico declared war on the Axis powers, and although the decision struck Irma Carrasco as a blunder, or at best a ridiculous joke, she was, above all, a Mexican, so she decided to return to Spain and await further developments.

In 1946, the day after the première of her play *The Moon in her Eyes*, which was greeted with discreet enthusiasm by the critics and the public, there was a knock at the door of her simple but comfortable apartment in Lavapiés. It was Barreda, reappearing on the scene.

The architect, who was living in New York, had come to make a new start. On his knees, he begged forgiveness, and made all the promises and oaths that Irma was longing to hear. The embers of their first love were rekindled. Irma's tender heart did the rest.

They returned to America. Barreda had, indeed, changed.

During the voyage he was tirelessly attentive and affectionate. The ship on which they had embarked in Europe took them to New York. Barreda's apartment on Third Avenue had been specially prepared for Irma's arrival. Their second honeymoon lasted three months. In New York, Irma experienced moments of great happiness. They decided to have children as soon as possible, but Irma did not get pregnant.

In 1947, the couple returned to Mexico. Barreda took up with his old friends, seeing them every day. Those friends or the air of Mexico City transformed him: he reverted to his former self, the fearsome husband of the bad old days. His behavior became erratic; he started drinking again and seeing chorus girls; he stopped listening and talking to his wife. Soon the verbal abuse began, and one night, after Irma, in conversation with some friends, had defended the honor of Franco's regime and praised its achievements, Barreda hit her.

The initial relapse into conjugal violence was immediately followed by a rash of similar incidents, occurring almost daily. But Irma was writing and that was what saved her. In spite of beatings, insults and humiliations of all sorts, she persisted in her work, holed up in a room of her house in Coyoacán, while Barreda succumbed to alcohol and the Mexican Communist Party's endless internal debates. In 1948, Irma finished *Juan Diego*, a strange and subtle play in which the Indian who saw the Virgin of Guadalupe and his guardian angel make their way through Purgatory, on what seems to be an eternal journey, since Purgatory itself, the author seems to be suggesting, is eternal. After the premiere Salvador Novo came backstage to congratulate Irma. He kissed her hand and they exchanged elaborate compliments. Meanwhile Barreda, who was talking or pretending to talk with some friends, watched her every move. He seemed increasingly nervous. Irma was taking on gigantic proportions in his eyes. He began to stutter and sweat profusely. In the end he completely lost control of the situation: shoving his way across the room, he insulted Novo and slapped Irma repeatedly, to the astonishment of the onlookers, who might have been quicker to separate husband and wife.

Three days later, Barreda was arrested, along with half of the Communist Party's Central Committee. Once again, Irma was free.

But she did not abandon Barreda. She visited him, took him books on architecture and detective novels, made sure that he was eating properly, had endless discussions with his lawyer, and looked after the running of his business. In Lecumberri, where he spent six months, Barreda quarreled with the other Communist prisoners, who found out for themselves just how hard it could be to share a confined space for a long time with a man of his temperament. He narrowly escaped summary justice at the hands of his comrades. On his release from prison, he quit the Party, publicly abjured his former activism, and left for New York with Irma. Everything seemed to bode well: they would begin a new life, once again. Irma was confident that, away from Mexico, their marriage would recover its former happiness and harmony. It was not to be: Barreda was embittered and he took it out on Irma. Life in New York, where they had known such joy, became hellish, and one morning Irma decided to leave it all behind. She took the first bus she could find, and three days later she was back in Mexico.

They would not see each other again until 1952. In the meantime, Irma had two new plays staged, *Carlotta, Empress of Mexico* and *The Miracle of Peralvillo*, both of which dealt with religious themes. She also published her first novel, *Vulture Hill*, a recreation of the last days in the life of her only brother. The book divided the critics in Mexico. According to some, Irma's message was that the only way to save the country from impending disaster was simply to turn the clock back to 1899. For others, *Vulture Hill* was an apocalyptic novel prefiguring the disasters awaiting the nation, which no one could forestall or counteract. The Vulture Hill of the title, where her brother, Father Joaquín María (whose reflections and memories occupy the greater part of the text), was executed, represents the future geography of Mexico: barren, desolate, a perfect scene for further crimes. The firing squad's commanding officer, Captain Álvarez, represents the PRI, the governing party steering the nation towards disaster. The soldiers of the firing squad are the misguided, dechristianized Mexican people, imperturbably attending their own funeral. A journalist from a Mexico City newspaper represents the country's intellectuals: hollow, faithless individuals, interested only in money. The old priest, disguised as a farmer, watching the execution from a distance, exemplifies the attitude of Mother Church, exhausted and terrified by the violence of mankind. The Greek traveling salesman, Yorgos Karantonis, who learns of the execution in the village and climbs the hill out of curiosity, simply to kill time, is the incarnation of hope: Karantonis falls to his knees weeping as Father Joaquín María is riddled with bullets. And, finally, the children who are playing on the other side of the hill, facing away from the execution, throwing stones at each other, represent Mexico's future: civil war and ignorance.

"The only political system in which I have complete confidence," she told an interviewer from the women's magazine

*Housework*, "is theocracy, although Generalísimo Franco is doing a pretty good job too."

The literati of Mexico, almost without exception, turned their backs on her.

In 1953, after another reconciliation with Barreda, who had become a renowned architect, the couple traveled to the Orient: Hawaii, Japan, the Philippines and India inspired Irma to write the new poems of *The Virgin of Asia*, steely sonnets fearlessly probing the open wound of modernity. The solution, it now seemed to her, was to return to sixteenth-century Spain.

In 1955 she was hospitalized with various broken bones and extensive bruising.

Barreda, now a self-declared libertarian, had reached the height of his fame: his reputation as an architect was international and commissions from all over the world came flooding into his firm. Irma, by contrast, gave up writing plays and dedicated herself to her house, the social life she led with her husband, and the painstaking construction of a poetic work that would only come to light after her death. In 1960 Barreda tried to divorce her for the first time. Irma refused, using all the resources at her disposal. A year later Barreda walked away from the marriage, leaving the matter in the hands of his lawyers, who put pressure on Irma, threatening to cut off the money and create a public scandal, appealing to her common sense, and her good heart (the woman with whom Barreda was living in Los Angeles was about to have a child), but to no avail.

In 1963, Barreda visited her for the last time. Irma was ill, and it is not entirely unreasonable to suppose that the architect was moved by pity, or curiosity, or some such sentiment.

Irma received him in the lounge, wearing her best suit. Barreda had come with his two-year-old son; outside, waiting in the car, was his new woman, a North American twenty years younger than Irma, and six months pregnant. Their final meeting was tense and, at certain moments, dramatic. Barreda inquired about Irma's health, and even about her poetry. Are you still writing? he asked. Irma replied gravely in the affirmative. Barreda was at first bothered and inhibited by the presence of his son. Then he recovered his nerve and adopted a distant tone, which gradually became more ironic and covertly aggressive. When he mentioned the lawyers and the necessity of obtaining a divorce, Irma looked him in the eye (him and his son) and flatly refused once again. Barreda did not insist. I've come as a friend, he said. A friend? You? (Irma was regal.) You are my husband, not my friend, she declared. Barreda smiled. The years had mellowed him, or he was pretending they had, or perhaps Irma meant so little to him that he was not even annoyed. The child did not move. Irma took pity on him and timidly suggested that he go and play on the patio. When they were alone, Barreda said something about how important it was for children to be raised by a proper married couple. What would you know, retorted Irma. True, admitted Barreda, what would I know. They drank. Barreda drank Sauza tequila, and Irma drank *rompope*. The boy played on the patio. Irma's servant, who was almost a child herself, played with him. In the half-light of the lounge, Barreda sipped his tequila and made banal remarks about the upkeep of the house, then announced that it was time for him to go. Irma got up first and, quick as a flash, refilled his glass. Let's drink a toast, she said. To us, said Barreda, to good luck. They looked each other in the eye. Barreda began to feel uncomfortable. Irma screwed up her lips in a grimace of contempt or irritation, and flung the glass of *rompope* onto the floor. It smashed, and the yellow liquid ran over the white tiles. Barreda, who for a moment thought she would throw the glass at his face, stared at her, surprised and alarmed. Hit me, said Irma. Go on, hit me, hit me, and she presented her body to him. Her cries grew louder and louder. Yet the child and the servant went on playing on the patio. Barreda watched them out of the corner of his eye: they seemed to be immersed in another time, no, in another dimension. Then he looked at Irma, and for a second he had a vague (and immediately forgotten) sense of what horror is. As he was walking out the front door with his son in his arms, he thought he could hear Irma's stifled cries coming from the lounge, where she was still standing, indifferent to everything but her last conjugal act, deaf to everything but her own voice softly repeating an invitation or an exorcism or a poem, the flayed part of a poem, shorter than any of Tablada's haikus, her only experimental poem, in a manner of speaking.

There were to be no more poems or little glasses of *rompope*, nothing but a religious, sepulchral silence until her death.

## DANIELA DE MONTECRISTO

*Buenos Aires, 1918–Córdoba, Spain, 1970*

Daniela de Montecristo was a woman of legendary beauty, surrounded by an enduring aura of mystery. The stories that have circulated about her first years in Europe (1938-1947) rarely concur and often flatly contradict one another. It has been said that among her lovers were Italian and German generals (including the infamous Wolff, SS and Police Chief in Italy); that she fell in love with a general in the Rumanian army, Eugenio Entrescu, who was crucified by his own soldiers in 1944; that she escaped from Budapest under siege disguised as a Spanish nun; that she lost a suitcase full of poems while secretly crossing the border from Austria into Switzerland in the company of three war criminals; that she had audiences with the Pope in 1940 and 1941; that out of unrequited love for her, a Uruguayan and then a Colombian poet committed suicide; and, that she had a black swastika tattooed on her left buttock.

Her literary work, leaving aside the juvenilia lost among the icy peaks of Switzerland, never to appear again, consists of a single book, with a rather epic title: *The Amazons*, published by Quill Argentina, with a preface by the widow Mendiluce, who could not be accused of restraint when it came to lavishing praise (in one paragraph, relying solely on her feminine intuition, she compared the legendary poems lost in the Alps to the work of Juana de Ibarbourou and Alfonsina Storni).

*The Amazons* is a torrential and anarchic blend of all the literary genres: romance, spy novel, memoir, play (there are even some passages of avant-garde dramatic writing), poetry, history, political pamphlet. The plot revolves around the life of the author and her grandmothers and great-grandmothers, sometimes going back as far as the period immediately following the foundation of Asunción and Buenos Aires.

The book contains some original passages, especially the descriptions of the Women's Fourth Reich—with its headquarters in Buenos Aires and its training grounds in Patagonia—and the nostalgic, pseudo-scientific digressions about a gland that produces the feeling of love.

# TWO GERMANS AT THE
# ENDS OF THE EARTH

## FRANZ ZWICKAU

### Caracas, 1946–Caracas, 1971

Franz Zwickau tore through life and literature like a whirlwind. The son of German immigrants, he was perfectly fluent in his parents' language as well as that of his native land. Contemporary reports portray him as a talented, iconoclastic boy who refused to grow up (José Segundo Heredia once described him as "Venezuela's best schoolboy poet"). The photos show a tall young man with blond hair, the body of an athlete, and the gaze of a killer or a dreamer or both.

He published two books of poetry. The first, *Motorists* (1965), was a series of twenty-five sonnets, rather unorthodox in their rhythm and form, dealing with subjects dear to the young: motorcycles, doomed love, sexual awakening and the will to purity. The second, *The War Criminals' Son* (1967), marked a substantial shift in Zwickau's poetics and, it could be said, in the Venezuelan poetry of the time. A dire, horrifying, badly written book (Zwickau espoused a peculiar theory about the revision of poems, somewhat surprising in a poet who had cut his teeth on sonnets), full of insults, imprecation, blasphemy, completely false autobiographical details, slanderous imputations, and nightmares.

A number of the poems are noteworthy:

—"A Dialogue with Hermann Goering in Hell," in which the poet, astride the black motorcycle of his early sonnets, arrives at an abandoned airfield, in a place known as Hell, near Maracaibo on the Venezuelan coast, and meets the shade of the Reichsmarschall, with whom he discusses various subjects: aviation, vertigo, destiny, uninhabited houses, courage, justice and death.

—"Concentration Camp," by contrast, is the humorous and at times touching story of Zwickau's life as a child, between the ages of five and ten, in a middle-class neighborhood of Caracas.

—"Heimat" (350 lines), written in an odd blend of Spanish and German—with occasional expressions in Russian, English, French and Yiddish—describes the private parts of his body with the detachment of a pathologist working in a morgue the night after a multiple murder.

—"The War Criminals' Son," the book's long title poem, is a vigorous and excessive piece, in which Zwickau, bemoaning the fact that he was born twenty-five years too late, gives free rein to his verbal facility, his hatred, his humor, and his unrelieved pessimism. In free verse of a kind rarely seen in Venezuela, the author depicts an appalling, indescribable childhood, compares himself to a black boy in Alabama in 1858, dances, sings, masturbates, lifts weights, dreams of a fabulous Berlin, recites Goethe and Jünger, attacks Montaigne and Pascal (whose work he knows well), adopting the voices of an alpine mountaineer, a peasant woman, a German tanker in Peiper's brigade who was killed in the Ardennes in December 1944, and a North American journalist in Nuremberg.

Needless to say, the collection was ignored, perhaps in a deliberate and concerted manner, by the influential critics of the day.

For a brief period, Zwickau joined Segundo José Heredia's literary circle. His active participation in the Aryan Naturist Community gave rise to his only work in prose, the short novel *Prison Camping*, in which he mercilessly lampoons the community's founder (who is clearly the model for Camacho, the Rosenberg of the Plains) and his disciples, the Pure Mestizos.

His relations with the literary world were always problematic. Only two anthologies of Venezuelan poetry include his work: *New Poetic Voices* (1966), edited by Alfredo Cuervo, and Fanny Arespacochea's controversial *Young Poets of Venezuela 1960-1970*.

Before his twenty-fifth birthday, Zwickau went over the edge of the Camino de Los Teques in Caracas on his motorbike. The poems he had written in German only came to light posthumously: entitled *Meine Kleine Gedichte*, the collection contains fifty brief texts in a more or less bucolic vein.

WILLY SCHÜRHOLZ

*Colonia Renacer, Chile, 1956–Kampala, Uganda, 2029*

Colonia Renacer (literally "Rebirth Colony") is twenty-five miles from Temuco. At first glance it seems to be a large estate like many others in the region. A closer look, however, reveals a number of significant differences. To begin with, Colonia Renacer has its own school, medical clinic, and auto repair shop. It has established a self-sufficient economic system that allows the colony to turn its back on what Chileans, perhaps over-optimistically, like to call "Chilean reality," or simply "reality." Colonia Renacer is a profitable business. Its presence is unsettling: the colony's members hold their festivities in secret; no neighbors, be they rich or poor, are invited. The colonists bury their dead in their own cemetery. A final differentiating trait, perhaps the most trivial but also the first to strike those who have caught a glimpse of the colony's interior and the few who have crossed its perimeter, is the ethnic origin of its inhabitants: they are all, without exception, German.

They work communally, from sunrise to sunset. They do not hire laborers or lease portions of their land. Superficially they resemble the many Protestant sects that emigrated from Germany to the Americas, fleeing intolerance and military service. But they are not a religious sect, and their arrival in Chile coincided with the end of the Second World War.

Every so often the national newspapers report their activities, or describe the mystery in which they are enveloped. There has been talk of pagan orgies, sex slaves and secret executions. Eye-witnesses of dubious reliability have sworn that in the main courtyard, instead of the Chilean colors, a red flag is flown, with a white circle in which a black swastika is inscribed. It has also been said that Eichman, Bormann and Mengele were hidden there. In fact the only war criminal to have spent time in the colony (a number of years in fact, entirely given over to horticulture) was Walther Rauss, who, it was later claimed, had taken a part in certain torture sessions during the early years of Pinochet's regime. The truth is that Rauss died of a heart attack while watching a soccer match on television: East and West Germany playing in the Federal Republic during the 1974 World Cup.

It was said that inbreeding in the colony produced idiot children and freaks. Neighbors used to speak of albino families driving tractors at night, and magazine articles of the time contain what are probably manipulated photos in which the dismayed Chilean public was able to examine a number of rather pale and serious individuals tirelessly working the fields.

After the coup in 1973, Colonia Renacer disappeared from the news.

Willy Schürholz, the youngest of five brothers, did not learn to speak Spanish properly until he was ten years old. Until then his world was the vast domain enclosed by the colony's barbed-wire fences. Unbending family discipline, farm work, and a series of singular teachers inspired equally by national-socialist millenarianism and by faith in science forged his character: withdrawn, stubborn and strangely self-confident.

It so happened that his elders decided to send him to Santiago to study agricultural science, and there he soon discovered his true poetic vocation. He had what it takes to fail spectacularly: even his earliest works have a discernible style of their own, an aesthetic direction that he would follow with hardly a deviation until the day he died. Schürholz was an experimental poet.

His first poems combined disconnected sentences and topographic maps of Colonia Renacer. They were untitled. They were unintelligible. Their aim was not to be understood, and certainly not to secure the reader's complicity. One critic has suggested that they indicate where to dig for the buried treasure of a lost childhood. Another maliciously surmised that they show the locations of secret graves. Schürholz's friends from the avant-garde poetry scene, who were generally opposed to the military regime, gave him the affectionate nickname The Treasure Map, until they discovered that he espoused ideas diametrically opposed to their own. The discovery took some time. No one could have accused Schürholz of being talkative.

In Santiago he lived in extreme poverty and solitude. He had no friends or lovers as far as we know; he avoided human contact. The little money that he earned by translating from German went to pay for his boarding-house room and a few hot meals each month. His diet consisted mainly of whole-wheat bread.

His second series of poetic experiments, which he exhibited in one up the literature department's classrooms at the Catholic University, was a series of huge maps which took some time to decipher, on which verses giving further instructions for their placement and use had been written in a careful, adolescent hand. A mass of gibberish. According to a professor of Italian literature who was well versed in the subject, they were maps of the concentration camps at Terezin, Mauthausen, Auschwitz, Bergen-Belsen, Buchenwald and Dachau. The installation remained in place for four days (instead of the planned week) and disappeared without having reached the attention of a wide public. Among those who saw and were able to interpret it, opinions differed: some said it was a critique of the military regime; others, influenced by Schürholz's erstwhile avant-garde friends, regarded it as a serious and criminal proposal to reconstruct the dismantled camps in Chile. The scandal, though minor, indeed almost confidential, was enough to endow Schürholz with the dark aura of the *poète maudit*, which would shadow him all the rest of his days.

The *Review of Thought and History* published his less explicit texts and maps. In certain circles he was considered the only disciple of the enigmatic, vanished Ramírez Hoffman, although the young man from Colonia Renacer lacked the master's excess: his art was systematic, monothematic and concrete.

In 1980, with the support of the *Review of Thought and History*, he published his first book. Füchler, the editor of the review, wanted to write a preface. Schürholz refused. The book is called

*Geometry*, and it sets out countless variations on the theme of a barbed-wire fence crossing an almost empty space, sparsely scattered with apparently unrelated verses. The fences seen from the air trace precise and delicate lines. The verses speak— or whisper—of an abstract pain, the sun and headaches.

The subsequent books were called *Geometry II*, *Geometry III* and so on. They return to the same theme: maps of concentration camps superimposed on a map of Colonia Renacer, or a particular city (Stutthof or Valparaíso, Maidanek or Concepción), or situated in an empty, rural space. Over the years, the textual component gradually became more consistent and clear. The disjointed sentences gave way to fragments of conversations about time or landscape, passages from plays in which, apparently, nothing is happening, except the slow, fluid passing of the years.

In 1985, Schürholz, whose fame had previously been restricted to Chile's literary and artistic circles, vast as they are, was catapulted to the very summit of notoriety by a group of local and North American impresarios. Commanding a team of excavators, he dug the map of an ideal concentration camp into the Atacama desert: an intricate network which, from the ground, appeared to be an ominous series of straight lines, but viewed from a helicopter or an airplane resolved into a graceful set of curves. The poet himself dispatched the literary component by inscribing the five vowels with a hoe and a mattock at locations scattered arbitrarily over the terrain's rugged surface. This performance was soon hailed in Chile as the cultural sensation of the summer.

The experiment was repeated in the Arizona desert and a wheat field in Colorado, with significant variations. Schürholz's eager promoters wanted to find him a light plane so he could draw a concentration camp in the sky, but he refused: his ideal camps were meant to be observed from the sky, but they could only be drawn on the earth. Thus he missed another opportunity to emulate and outdo Ramírez Hoffman.

It soon became apparent that Schürholz was neither competitive nor concerned with his career. Interviewed by a New York television station, he came across as a fool. Haltingly, he declared that he knew nothing about the visual arts, and hoped to learn to write one day. His humility was charming for a while but soon became ridiculous.

In 1990, to the surprise of his followers, he published a book of children's stories, using the futile pseudonym Gaspar Hauser. Within a few days all the critics knew that Gaspar Hauser was Willy Schürholz, and the children's stories were scrutinized with disdain and pitilessly dissected. In his stories, Hauser-Schürholz idealized a childhood that was suspiciously aphasic, amnesic, obedient and silent. Invisibility seemed to be his aim. In spite of the critics, the book sold well. Schürholz's main character, "the boy without a name," displaced Papelucho as the emblematic protagonist of children's and teen fiction in Chile.

Shortly afterwards, amid protests from certain sectors of the left, Schürholz was offered the position of cultural attaché to the Chilean Embassy in Angola, which he accepted. In Africa he found what he had been looking for: the fitting repository for his soul. He never returned to Chile. He spent the rest of his life working as a photographer and as a guide for German tourists.

# SPECULATIVE AND
# SCIENCE FICTION

# J.M.S. HILL

*Topeka, 1905–New York, 1936*

One of Quantrill's Raiders crossing the state of Kansas at the head of 500 cavalrymen; flags inscribed with a sort of primitive, premonitory swastika; rebels who never surrender; a plan to reach Great Bear Lake via Kansas, Nebraska, South Dakota, North Dakota, Saskatchewa, Alberta, and the Northwest Territories; a Confederate philosopher whose fanciful dream was to establish an Ideal Republic in the vicinity of the Arctic circle; an expedition unraveling along the way, beset by human and natural obstacles; two exhausted horsemen finally reaching Great Bear Lake, dismounting. . . . Such, in summary, is the plot of J.M.S. Hill's first novel, published in 1924 in the *Fantastic Stories* series.

Between then and his premature death twelve years later, Hill was to publish more than thirty novels and more than fifty stories.

His characters are usually based on figures from the Civil War and sometimes even bear their names (General Ewell, Early, the lost explorer in *The Early Saga*, young Jeb Stuart in *The World of Snakes*, the journalist Lee); the action unfolds in a distorted present where nothing is as it seems, or in a distant future full of abandoned, ruined cities, and ominously silent landscapes, similar in many respects to those of the Midwest. His plots abound in providential heroes and mad scientists; hidden clans and tribes which at the ordained time must emerge and do battle with other hidden tribes; secret societies of men in black who meet at isolated ranches on the prairie; private detectives who must search for people lost on other planets; children stolen and raised by inferior races so that, having reached adulthood, they may take control of the tribe and lead it to immolation; unseen animals with insatiable appetites; mutant plants; invisible planets that suddenly become visible; teenage girls offered as human sacrifices; cities of ice with a single inhabitant; cowboys visited by angels; mass migrations destroying everything in their path; underground labyrinths swarming with warrior-monks; plots to assassinate the president of the United States; spaceships fleeing an earth in flames to colonize Jupiter; societies of telepathic killers; children growing up all alone in dark, cold yards.

Hill's writing is not pretentious. His characters speak as people no doubt spoke in Topeka in 1918. His infinite enthusiasm makes up for occasional stylistic sloppiness.

J.M.S. Hill was the youngest of four sons born to an Episcopalian minister and his wife. His mother was loving, given to daydreaming, and before her marriage had worked in the box office of a cinema in her home town. After leaving home, Hill lived mostly alone. He is known to have had only one, unhappy, love affair. He rarely discussed his personal life in public, stating that he was, above all, a professional writer. In private he boasted about having designed part of the Nazi uniform and kit, although it is most unlikely that his inventions were known so far afield.

His novels are full of heroes and titans. The settings are desolate, vast and cold. He wrote Wild West novels and detective books, but he did his best work in science fiction. A number of his books combine all three genres. At the age of twenty-five, he moved into a little apartment in New York City, where he was to die six years later. Among his belongings was an unfinished novel on a pseudo-historical subject, *The Fall of Troy*, which would not be published until 1954.

## ZACH SODENSTERN

*Los Angeles, 1962–Los Angeles, 2021*

A highly successful science fiction writer, Zach Soden-stern was the creator of the Gunther O'Connell saga, of the Fourth Reich saga, and of the saga of Gun-ther O'Connell and the Fourth Reich, in which the previous two sagas fuse into one (Gunther O'Connell, the West Coast gangster turned politician, having successfully infiltrated the underworld of the Fourth Reich in the Midwest).

The first and second sagas comprise more than ten novels, while the third is made up of three, one of them unfinished. Some of the stories are particularly worthy of note. *A Little House in Napa* (the beginning of the Gunther O'Connell saga) is set in a world of extreme violence perpetrated by chil-dren and teenagers, described in a restrained manner, without spelling out moral lessons or suggesting any solutions to the problems. The novel appears to be a mere succession of unpleasant situations and acts of aggression, interrupted only by the words THE END. At first glance it does not seem to be a work of science fiction. Only the dreams or visions of the adolescent Gunther O'Connell give it a certain prophetic, fantastic coloring. No space voyages, robots or scientific advances figure in its pages. On the contrary, the society it describes seems to have regressed to an inferior degree of civilization.

*Candace* (1990) is the second installment of the Gunther O'Connell saga. The adolescent protagonist has become a twenty-five-year-old determined to change his life and the lives of others. The novel recounts the ins and outs of his job as a construction worker, and his love for a slightly older woman called Candace, who is married to a corrupt policeman. The opening pages introduce the reader to O'Connell's dog, a mutant, stray German Shepherd with telepathic powers and Nazi tendencies; in the last fifty pages it becomes clear that a major earthquake has occurred in California and that the United States government has been toppled by a coup.

*Revolution* and *The Crystal Cathedral* are the third and fourth installments of the saga. *Revolution* consists basically of dialogues between O'Connell and his dog Flip plus various secondary episodes of extreme violence set in a ruined Los Angeles. *The Crystal Cathedral* is a story about God, fundamentalist preachers and the ultimate meaning of life. Sodenstern portrays O'Connell as a calm but withdrawn man, who carries the skull of his great lost love Candace (who was killed by her husband in the second novel of the cycle) in a little bag permanently attached to his belt, nostalgically remembers various old TV series (in suspiciously accurate detail), and is friend to no one but his dog, who has taken on an increas-

ingly important role: Flip's adventures and reflections constitute sub-novels within the novel.

*The Cephalopods* and *Warriors of the South* cap off the
O'Connell saga. *The Cephalopods* records O'Connell's trip
to San Francisco with Flip and their adventures in that city
(where gays and lesbians rule supreme). *Warriors of the South*
relates the clash between earthquake survivors in California
and millions of hungry Mexicans marching northward en
masse, devouring everything in their path. The situation is
reminiscent, at times, of the conflict between Romans and
barbarians on the fringes of the Empire.

*Checking the Maps* opens the Fourth Reich saga. It is full
of appendices, maps, incomprehensible indices of proper
names, and solicits an interaction in which no sensible reader
would persist. The events take places mainly in Denver and
Midwestern cities. There is no main character. The less chaotic stretches read like collections of stories haphazardly
tacked together. *Our Friend B* and *The Ruins of Pueblo* con-
tinue in the same vein. The characters are designated by letters or numbers, and the texts are not so much scrambled
puzzles as *fragments* of scrambled puzzles. Although presented
and sold as a novel, *The Fourth Reich in Denver* is in fact a
reader's guide to the three preceding titles. *The Simbas*—the
last installment before the confluence of the Fourth Reich and
O'Connell sagas—a surreptitious manifesto directed against
African Americans, Jews and Hispanics, gave rise to diverse
and contradictory interpretations.

Sodenstern was a cult author, and several of his novels had
been adapted for the screen by the time he came to publish the
last three, which recount Gunther O'Connell's initiatory voyage toward the central territories of the American continent

and his subsequent encounter with the mysterious leaders of the Fourth Reich. In *The Bat-Gangsters*, O'Connell and Flip cross the Rockies. In *Anita*, an aging O'Connell rediscovers love with a teenage replica of his old girlfriend Candace (the plot is a simple transposition of Sodenstern's situation at the time: he was besotted, like a teenager, with a young UCLA student). And in *A,* O'Connell finally penetrates to the heart of the Fourth Reich, of which he is elected leader.

According to Sodenstern's plans, the saga of O'Connell and the Fourth Reich was to comprise five novels. Of the final two only rough outlines and indecipherable lists have survived. The fourth, to be entitled *The Arrival*, would have narrated a long vigil: O'Connell, Flip, Anita and the members of the Fourth Reich awaiting the birth of a new Messiah. The final, untitled novel would probably have explored the consequences of the Messiah's coming. In a file on his computer, Sodenstern noted that that the Messiah could be Flip's son, but there is nothing to suggest that this was more than verbal doodling.

## GUSTAVO BORDA

### *Guatemala, 1954–Los Angeles, 2016*

Guatemala's most talented and unfortunate science-fiction writer spent his childhood and teenage years in the countryside. His father was the overseer of an estate called Los Laureles, whose owners had a library, and there it was that Gustavo learned to read and first tasted humiliation. Both reading and humiliation were to be constant features of his life.

Borda preferred blondes, and his insatiable libido was legendary, provoking innumerable jokes and jeers. Given the ease with which he fell in love and took offense, his life was one long series of indignities, which he endured with the fortitude of a wounded beast. Anecdotes about his life in California abound (yet there are few about his life in Guatemala, where he came to be regarded, albeit briefly, as the nation's great writer): it is said that he was a favorite target for all the sadists in Hollywood; that he fell in love with at least five actresses, four secretaries, and seven waitresses, every one of whom rejected him, deeply wounding his pride; that on more that one occasion he was brutally beaten up by the brothers, friends, or lovers of the woman in question; that his own friends took pleasure in getting him catatonically drunk and leaving him lying in a heap, wherever; that he was fleeced by his agent, his landlord, and his neighbor (the Mexican screenwriter and science-fiction author Alfredo de María); that his presence at meetings and conferences of North American science-fiction writers was a source of sarcastic, scornful amusement (Borda, as opposed to the majority of his colleagues, had not even a rudimentary knowledge of science; his ignorance in the fields of astronomy, astrophysics, quantum theory and information technology was proverbial); that his mere existence, in short, brought out the basest, most deeply hidden instincts in the people whose paths he crossed, for one reason or another, in the course of his life.

There is, however, no evidence to suggest that any of this demoralized him. In his *Diaries* he blames the Jews and usurers for everything.

Gustavo Borda was just over five feet tall; he had a swarthy complexion, thick black hair, and enormous very white teeth. His characters, by contrast, are tall, fair-haired and blue-eyed. The spaceships that appear in his novels have German names. Their crews are German too. The colonies in space are called New Berlin, New Hamburg, New Frankfurt, and New Koenigsberg. His cosmic police dress and behave like SS officers who have somehow managed to survive into the twenty-second century.

In other respects, Borda's plots are entirely conventional:

young men setting off on initiatory voyages; children lost in the immensity of the cosmos who encounter wise old navigators; stories of Faustian pacts with the devil; planets where the fount of eternal youth may be found; lost civilizations surviving in secret. . . .

He lived in Guatemala City and in Mexico, where he worked at all sorts of jobs. His first books went entirely unnoticed.

After the translation of his fourth novel, *Unsolved Crimes in Force-City*, into English, he became a professional writer, and moved to Los Angeles, where he was to spend the rest of his life.

In answer to a question about the puzzling abundance of Germanic elements in the work of a Central American author, he once said: "I have been tormented, spat on, and deceived so often—the only way I could go on living and writing was to find spiritual refuge in an ideal place . . . In a way, I'm like a woman trapped in a man's body. . . ."

# MAGICIANS, MERCENARIES AND MISERABLE CREATURES

## Segundo José Heredia

*Caracas, 1927–Caracas, 2004*

A man of impetuous and passionate character, the young Segundo José Heredia was nicknamed Socrates because of his insatiable appetite for discussion and debate on all manner of topics. He preferred to compare himself, however, to Richard Burton and T.E. Lawrence, for like those authors, he too wrote tales of adventure, three to begin with: *Sergeant P* (1955), the story of a Waffen SS veteran lost in the Venezuelan jungle, where he offers his services to a community of missionary nuns in permanent conflict with the government, as well as with local Indians and adventurers; *Night Signals* (1956), a novel about the dawn of Venezuelan aviation, the research for which included learning not only to fly a prop plane but also to parachute; and *The Confession of the Rose* (1958), in which, forgoing the vast spaces of the Fatherland, the author confines the adventure to a mental hospital, and in fact to the patients' minds, making abundant use of interior monologue, diverse points of view, and a forensic-medical jargon that was widely admired at the time.

In the following years he traveled around the world several times, directed two films and gathered around him in Caracas a group of young writers and critics, with whom he founded the magazine *Second Round*, a bimonthly devoted to the arts and certain sports (mountain climbing, boxing, rugby, football, horse racing, baseball, track and field, swimming, hunting, and game fishing) which were always examined from the writer's or adventurer's point of view, by the finest stylists Segundo José Heredia could muster.

In 1970 he published his fourth and final novel, which he considered his masterpiece: *Saturnalia*, the story of two young friends, who in the course of a week-long journey through France are confronted with the most horrendous acts they have ever witnessed, without being able to tell for sure whether or not they are dreaming. The novel includes scenes of rape, sexual and workplace sadism, incest, impaling, and human sacrifice in prisons crowded to the physical limit; there are convoluted murder plots in the tradition of Conan Doyle, colorful and realistic descriptions of every Paris neighborhood, and, incidentally, one of the most vivid and spine-chilling female characters in Venezuelan literature since 1950: Elisenda, the enemy of the two young men.

*Saturnalia* was banned for some time in Venezuela, and later reissued by two South American publishers, before lapsing into oblivion, with the author's apparent consent.

In the sixties he founded the short-lived Aryan Naturist

Commune (or "nudist colony," as its detractors called it) near Calabozo, in the state of Guárico.

In his final years he attached little importance to his day-to-day life and none at all to his literary works.

## AMADO COUTO

*Juiz de Fora, Brazil, 1948–Paris, 1989*

Couto wrote a book of stories, which all the publishers rejected. The manuscript went astray. Then he began work with the death squads, kidnapping, participating in torture and witnessing the killing of certain prisoners, but he went on thinking about literature, and specifically what it was that Brazilian literature needed. It needed avant-garde, experimental writing, a real shake-up, but not like the Campos brothers, they were boring, a pair of insipid professors, and not like Osman Lins, who was downright unreadable. (Why did they publish Osman Lins and not Couto's stories?) No, something modern but more up his alley, a kind of crime thriller (Brazilian, though, not North American), a new Rubem Fonseca, in a word. Now there was a good writer; he was rumored to be a son of a bitch, but Couto was keeping an open mind. One day, while he was waiting in a field with the car, he had an idea:

why not kidnap Fonseca and give him a going-over. He told his superiors and they listened. But the idea never came to fruition. Couto's dreams were clouded and illuminated by the possibility of making Fonseca the focus of a real-life novel. The superiors had superiors in turn and somewhere up the chain of command Fonseca's name evaporated—disappeared—but in the chain of Couto's thoughts, the name continued to grow and accrue prestige, opening itself to his thrust, as if the name Fonseca were a wound and the name Couto a knife. He read Fonseca, he read the wound until it began to suppurate; then he fell ill and his colleagues took him to hospital, where they say he became delirious: he saw the great Brazilian crime thriller in a hepatology unit; he saw it in detail, the plot complete with set-up and resolution, and he saw himself in the Egyptian desert approaching the unfinished pyramids like a wave (he *was* the wave). So he wrote the novel and had it published. Entitled *Nothing to Say*, it was a crime thriller. The hero was called Paulinho. Sometimes Paulinho worked for certain gentlemen as a chauffeur, sometimes he was a detective, and sometimes he was a skeleton smoking in a corridor, listening to distant cries, a skeleton who visited every dwelling (no, in fact only middle-class dwellings and those of the seriously poor) but never came too close to the inhabitants. The novel was published on the Black Pistol list, which was made up of North American, French and Brazilian thrillers, the proportion of local titles having risen as funds to buy foreign rights ran short. His colleagues read the novel and almost all of them found it incomprehensible. By then they were no longer cruising in the car or kidnapping and torturing, although they did still occasionally kill. I have to dissociate myself from these people and be a writer, Couto wrote. But he was conscientious. Once he tried to meet Fonseca. According to Couto, they looked at each other. And Couto thought: He's so old; he's not Mandrake any more, or anybody else. But he would gladly have changed places with Fonseca, if only for a week. He also thought that Fonseca's gaze was harder than his own. I live among pirañas, he wrote, but Don Rubem Fonseca lives in a tank full of metaphysical sharks. He wrote a letter to his hero, but received no reply. So he wrote another novel, *The Last Word*, published by Black Pistol, in which the return of Paulinho is a pretext for Couto to bare his soul to Fonseca, shamelessly, as if saying, Here I am, alone with my pirañas, while my colleagues drive around the city center in the small hours of the morning, like the Tonton Macoute who come to take bad children away . . . such are the mysteries of literature. And although he probably knew that Fonseca would never read his novels, he went on writing. In *The Last Word* more skeletons appear. Paulinho is a skeleton almost all day long. His clients are skeletons. The people he talks to, fucks and eats with (although he usually eats alone) are also skeletons. And in the third novel, *The Mute Girl*, the major cities of Brazil are like enormous skeletons, while the villages are like little children's skeletons, and sometimes even the words are transformed into bones. After that Couto stopped writing. Someone told him that his colleagues from the patrol had begun to disappear, and fear took hold of him, or rather tightened its grip and entered his body. He tried to retrace his steps and find familiar faces, but everything had changed while he was writing. Certain strangers began to talk about his novels. One of them could have been Fonseca, but wasn't. I had him in the palm of my hand, he noted in his diary before disappearing like a dream. He had gone to Paris, where he hanged himself in a room at the Hôtel La Grèce.

# Carlos Hevia

*Montevideo, 1940–Montevideo, 2006*

Author of a monumental and largely unreliable biography of San Martín, in which, among other inaccuracies, the general is said to have been Uruguayan, Hevia also wrote stories, collected in the volume *Seas and Offices*, and two novels: *Jason's Prize*, a fable suggesting that life on Earth is the result of a disastrous intergalactic television game show; and *Montevideo—Buenos Aires*, a novel about friendship, full of exhaustive all-night conversations.

He worked in television journalism, discharging lowly tasks for the most part, with occasional stints as a producer.

For some years he lived in Paris, where he became acquainted with the theories espoused by *The Review of Contemporary History*, which were to make a deep and lasting impression on him. He was a friend of the French philosopher Étienne de Saint Étienne, whose work he translated.

HARRY SIBELIUS

*Richmond, 1949—Richmond, 2014*

Harry Sibelius was prompted to write one of the most complex and dense works of his day (and possibly also one of the most futile) by his reading of Norman Spinrad and Philip K. Dick, and perhaps also by reflecting on a story by Borges. The novel, since it is a novel and not a work of history, is simple in appearance. It is founded on the following supposition: Germany, in alliance with Italy, Spain and the Vichy government in France, defeats England in the autumn of 1941. In the summer of the following year, four million soldiers are mobilized in an attack on the Soviet Union, which capitulates in 1944, except for pockets of sporadic resistance in Siberia. In the spring of 1946, European troops attack the United States from the East, while Japan invades from the West. In the winter of the same year New York falls, then Boston, Washington, Richmond, San Francisco and Los Angeles. The infantry and German Panzers cross the Appalachians; the Canadians withdraw to the interior; the United States government shifts its seat to Kansas City; and defeat is imminent on every front. The capitulation takes place in 1948. Alaska, part of California and part of Mexico are handed over to Japan. The rest of North America is occupied by the Germans. Harry Sibelius perfunctorily explains all these developments in a ten-page introduction (which is in fact little more than a list of key dates to give the reader historical points of reference), entitled "A Bird's Eye View." Then the novel proper—*The True Son of Job*—begins: 1,333 pages darkly mirroring Arnold J. Toynbee's *Hitler's Europe*.

The structure of the book is modeled on the work of the English historian. The second introduction (which is in fact the real prologue) is entitled "The Elusiveness of History," exactly like Toynbee's prologue. The following sentence from Toynbee expresses one of the pivotal themes of Sibelius's introductory text: "The historian's view is conditioned, always and everywhere, by his own location in time and place; and, since time and place are continually changing, no history, in the subjective sense of the word, can ever be a permanent record that will tell the story, once for all, in a form that will be equally acceptable to readers in all ages, or even in all quarters of the Earth." Sibelius, of course, is animated by intentions of an entirely different nature. In the final analysis, the British professor's aim is to testify against crime and ignominy, lest we forget. The Virginian novelist seems to believe that "somewhere in time and space" the crime in question has definitively triumphed, so he proceeds to catalogue it.

The first part of Toynbee's book is entitled "The Political Structure of Hitler's Europe," which becomes, in Sibelius, "The Political Structure of Hitler's America." Both parts comprise six chapters, but where Toynbee's account is factual, only a distorted reflection of reality is perceptible in Sibelius's welter of stories. His characters, who sometimes seem to have stepped straight out of a Russian novel (*War and Peace* was one of his favorites) and sometimes to have escaped from an animated cartoon, move, speak and indeed live (although their lives have little continuity) in chapters that seem inhospitable to fiction, such as the fourth, "Administration," in which Sibelius imagines in detail life in (1) the incorporated territories, (2) the territories under a chief of civil administration, (3) the appended territories, (4) the occupied territories, and (5) the "zones of operation."

It is not unusual for Sibelius to spend twenty pages simply introducing a character, specifying his physical and moral traits, his tastes in food and sports, his ambitions and frustrations, after which the character vanishes, never to be mentioned again in the course of the novel; while others, who are barely given names, reappear over and over, in widely separated locations, engaged in dissimilar if not incompatible or mutually exclusive activities. The workings of the bureaucratic machinery are described implacably. The 250 pages of the fourth chapter of the second part, "Transport," subdivided into (a) Position of German Transport at the Outbreak of the War, (b) Effects of the Changing Military Situation on the German Transport Position, (c) German Methods of controlling Transport throughout America, and (d) German Organization of American Transport, are overwhelming for all but the specialist.

The stories are often borrowed, as are almost all the characters. In the third chapter of the second part, "Industry and Raw Materials," we find Hemingway's Harry Morgan and Robert Jordan, along with characters from Robert Heinlein and plot devices from *Reader's Digest*. In the seventh chapter, "Finance," section (b), "German Exploitation of Foreign Countries," the informed reader will recognize a series of characters (sometimes Sibelius doesn't even go to the trouble of changing their names!): Faulkner's Sartorius and the Snopes (in *"Reichkreditkassen"*); Walt Disney's Bambi, and Gore Vidal's John Cave and Myra Breckenridge (in "Seizure of Gold and Foreign Assets"); Scarlett O'Hara and Rhett Butler along with Gertrude Stein's Herslands and Dehnings (in "Occupation Costs and other Levies"), which led a caustic critic to wonder whether Sibelius was the only American who had read *The Making of Americans*; various characters from John Dos Passos, Capote's Holly Golightly, and Patricia Highsmith's Ripley, Charles Bruno and Guy Daniel Haines (in "Clearing Agreements"); Hammet's Sam Spade and Vonnegut's Eliot Rosewater, Howard Campbell and Bokonon (in "Manipulation of Exchange Rates"); and F. Scott Fitzgerald's Amory Blaine, Gatsby and Monroe Starr, along with poems by Robert Frost and Wallace Stevens, and the abstract, oblique, shadowy characters they imply (in "German Control over American Banking").

Sibelius's stories—the hundreds of stories that intersect willy-nilly, without apparently affecting one another, in *The True Son of Job*—are not guided by any principle, nor do they constitute an overall vision (as one New York critic absurdly supposed, comparing the book to *War and Peace*). The stories simply happen, period—produced by the sovereign power of chance unleashed, operating outside time and space, at the dawn of a new age, as it were, in which spatio-temporal perception is undergoing transformation and even becoming obsolete. When Sibelius explains the political, economic and military order of the new America, he is intelligible. When he expounds the new religious, racial, judicial and industrial order, he is objective and clear. Administration is his strength. But it is only when his characters and stories, be they borrowed or original, infiltrate and overrun the painstakingly assembled bureaucratic machinery that he reaches the summit of his narrative art. The best of Sibelius is to be found in his tangled, implacably unfolding stories.

And, from a literary point of view, that is all there is to be found.

After the publication of his novel, Sibelius withdrew from the literary scene as quietly as he had arrived. He wrote articles for various war games magazines and fanzines in the United States. And he helped to design a number of games: one based on the battle of Antietam, another based on Chancellorsville, an operational Gettysburg game, a tactical Wilderness 1864, a Shiloh, a Bull Run. . . .

# THE MANY MASKS OF
# MAX MIREBALAIS

MAX MIREBALAIS, alias *MAX KASIMIR, MAX VON HAUPTMAN, MAX LE GUEULE, JACQUES ARTIBONITO*

*Port-au-Prince, 1941–Les Cayes, 1998*

His real name was probably Max Mirebalais, al-though we will never know for sure. His first steps in literature remain mysterious: one day he turned up in a newspaper editor's office; the next, he was out on the streets, looking for stories, or more often running er-rands for the senior staff. In the course of his apprentice-ship, he was subjected to all the miseries and servitudes of Haitian journalism. But thanks to his determination, after two years, he rose to the position of assistant social colum-nist for the Port-au-Prince *Monitor*, and in that capacity, awed and puzzled, he attended parties and soirées held in the capital's grandest houses. There can be no doubt that as soon as he glimpsed that world, he wanted to belong to it. He soon realized that there were only two ways to achieve his aim: through violence, which was out of the question, since he was peaceable and timorous by nature, appalled by the mere sight of blood; or through literature, which is a surreptitious form of violence, a passport to respectability, and can, in certain young and sensitive nations, disguise the social climber's origins.

He opted for literature and decided to spare himself the difficult years of apprenticeship. His first poems, published in the *Monitor*'s cultural supplement, were copied from Aimé Césaire, and met with a rather negative reception from certain intellectuals in Port-au-Prince, who openly mocked the young poet.

His next exercises in plagiarism demonstrated that he had learned his lesson: this time the poet imitated was René Depestre, and the result, if not unanimous acclaim, was the respect of a number of professors and critics, who predicted a brilliant future for the neophyte.

He could have continued with Depestre, but Max Mirebalais was no fool; he decided to multiply his sources. With patient craftsmanship, sacrificing hours of sleep, he plagiarized Anthony Phelps and Davertige, and created his first heteronym: Max Kasimir, the cousin of Max Mirebalais, to whom he attributed poems borrowed from those who had ridiculed his first ventures into print: Philoctète, Morisseau and Legagneur, founding members of the Haiti Littéraire group. The poets Lucien Lemoine and Jean Dieudonné Garçon came in for the same treatment.

With the passage of time he became expert in the art of breaking down the work of another poet in order to make it his own. Vanity soon got the better of him and he tried to conquer the world. French poetry provided a boundless hunting ground, but he decided to start closer to home. His plan, noted somewhere in his papers, was to exhaust the expressive repertoire of *négritude*.

So, after expressing and exhausting more than twenty authors, whose collections, although extremely hard to come by, were placed at his disposal free of charge by the Apollinaire French Bookshop, he decided to let Mirebalais take charge of Georges Desportes and Edouard Glissant from Martinique, while Max Kasimir assumed responsibility for Flavien Ranaivo from Madagascar and Leopold-Sedhar Senghor from Senegal. In plagiarizing Senghor his art reached a summit of perfection: no one realized that the five poems that appeared in the *Monitor* in the second week of September 1971 signed Max Kasimir were texts that Senghor had published in *Hosties noires* (Seuil, 1948) and *Ethiopiques* (Seuil, 1956).

He came to the attention of the powerful. As a society columnist he went on covering the soirées of Port-au-Prince, with greater enthusiasm if anything, and now he was greeted by the hosts and introduced in various ways (much to the confusion of the less literary guests), as our treasured poet Max Mirebalais, or our beloved poet Max Kasimir or, as certain jovial military men used to say, our esteemed bard Kasimir Mirebalais. He did not have to wait long for his reward: he was offered the post of cultural attaché in Bonn, which he accepted. It was the first time he had left the country.

Life abroad turned out to be awful. After an unbroken series of illnesses that kept him hospitalized for more than three months, he decided to create a new heteronym: the half-German, half-Haitian poet Max von Hauptman. This time he copied Fernand Rolland, Pierre Vasseur-Decroix and Julien Dunilac, whom he presumed were little known in Haiti. From the manipulated, made-over, metamorphosed texts rose the figure of a bard who even-handedly explored and sang the magnificence of the Aryan and the Masai races. After three rejections, the poems were accepted by a Parisian publisher. Von Hauptman was an immediate success. So while Mirebalais spent his days enduring the boredom of his work at the embassy or undergoing endless medical tests, he was coming to be known, in certain Parisian literary circles, as the Caribbean's bizarre answer to Pessoa. Naturally no one (not even the poets who had been plagiarized, some of whom could well have come across the curious texts of von Hauptman) noticed the fraud.

Mirebalais, it seems, was excited by the idea of being a Nazi poet while continuing to espouse a certain kind of *négritude*. He decided to pursue von Hauptman's creative work in greater depth. He began by clarifying—or obscuring—his origins. Von Hauptman was not one of Mirebalais' heteronyms. Mirebalais was a heteronym of von Hauptman, whose father, so he said, had been a sergeant in Doenitz's submarine fleet, cast up on the Haitian coast, a Robinson stranded in a hostile land, protected by a few Masai who sensed that he was their friend. He married the prettiest of the Masai girls, and Max was born in 1944 (which was a lie: he was born in 1941, but fame had gone to his head, and since he was enhancing the truth, he thought he might as well take three years off his age). Predictably, the French did not believe him, but neither did they take exception to his outlandish claims. All poets invent their past, as the French know better than anyone. In Haiti, however, reactions were diverse. Some saw Mirebalais as a pathetic fool. Others promptly invented European fathers or grandfathers of their own: shipwrecked seamen from German, English or French vessels, adventurers gone astray in some corner of the island. Overnight, the Mirebalais-von Hauptman phenomenon spread like a virus through the island's ruling class. Von Hauptman's poems were published in Port-au-Prince, affirmations of Masai identity ran riot (in a country where Masai ancestry is so rare as to be probably non-existent) accompanied by legends and family histories. A pair of adepts of the New Protestant Church even tried their hand at plagiarizing the plagiarist, without much success.

Fame, however, is quick to perish in the tropics. By the time he returned from Europe, the von Hauptman craze had been forgotten. Those who wielded real power—the Duvalier dynasty, the few wealthy families and the army—had little time for the preoccupations of an idealized, bogus half-breed. Dazzled by the Haitian sun, Mirebalais was sad to discover that order and the struggle against Communism carried more weight than the Aryan race, the Masai race and their common destiny in the universal realm. But quite undeterred, he prepared himself to unleash another heteronym upon the world, in a gesture of defiance. And so Max Le Gueule was born: the crowning glory of the plagiarist's art, a concoction of poets from Quebec, Tunisia, Algeria, Morocco, Lebanon, Cameroon, The Congo, the Central African Republic and Nigeria (not to mention the Malian poet Siriman Cissoko and the Guinean Keita Fodeba, to whose works, kindly lent by the old manic-depressive owner of the Apollinaire French Bookshop, Mirebalais initially reacted with howls and later with trembling).

The result was excellent; the reception non-existent.

This time Mirebalais' pride was wounded; for some years he withdrew to the dwindling, spectral Society section of the *Monitor*, and was obliged to supplement his income by taking up an obscure position in the Haitian Telephone Company.

The years of relegation were also years of poetic labor. The works of Mirebalais multiplied, as did those of Kasimir, von Hauptman and Le Gueule. The poets gained in depth; the differences between them became more clearly marked (von Hauptman the bard of the Aryan race, a fanatical mulatto Nazi; Le Gueule the model of the practical man, hard-headed and militaristic; Mirebalais the lyrical poet, the patriot, calling forth the shades of Toussaint L'Ouverture, Dessalines and Christophe, while Kasimir celebrated *négritude*, the landscapes of the fatherland and mother Africa, and the rhythm of the tam-tams). The similarities emerged more clearly too: they were all passionately devoted to Haiti, order and the family. In religious matters there was some disagreement: while Mirebalais and Le Gueule were Catholic and reasonably tolerant, Kasimir practised voodoo rites, and the vaguely Protestant von Hauptman was definitely intolerant. Clashes among the heteronyms were organized (especially between von Hauptman and Le Gueule, who were always spoiling for a fight), followed by reconciliations. They interviewed one another. The *Monitor* published some of the interviews. It is not absurd to suppose that one night, in a moment of inspiration and ambition, Mirebalais dreamed of constituting the whole of contemporary Haitian poetry on his own.

Feeling that he had been pigeonholed as picturesque (and this in a context where all the literature officially sanctioned by the Haitian regime was picturesque to say the least), Mirebalais made one last bid for fame or respectability.

Literature, as it had been conceived in the nineteenth century, had ceased to be relevant to the public, he thought. Poetry was dying. The novel wasn't, but he didn't know how to write novels. There were nights when he cried with rage.

Then he began searching for a solution, and he didn't let up until he found one.

In the course of his long career as a society columnist, he had come across a young fellow who was an extraordinary guitarist. He was the lover of a police colonel and lived rough in the slums of Port-au-Prince. Mirebalais sought him out and became his friend, without a precise plan at first, simply for the pleasure of hearing him play. Then he suggested they form a musical duo. The young man accepted.

And so Mirebalais' last heteronym was born: Jacques Artibonito, composer and singer. His lyrics were plagiarized from Nacro Alidou, a poet from Upper Volta, Germany's Gottfried Benn, and the Frenchman Armand Lanoux. The arrangements were the work of the guitarist, Eustache Descharnes, who ceded his copyright, in exchange for God knows what.

The duo's career was uneven. Mirebalais had a bad voice but insisted on singing. He had no sense of rhythm but insisted on dancing. They made a record. Eustache, who followed him everywhere with an utterly resigned docility, seemed more like a zombie than a guitarist. Together they toured all the venues in the country, from Port-au-Prince to Cap-Haïtien, from Gonaîves to Leogane. After two years, they could only get dates in the dingiest dives. One night Eustache hanged himself in the hotel room he was sharing with Mirebalais. The poet spent a week in prison until the death was declared a suicide. He received death threats on his release. Eustache's colonel friend promised publicly to teach him a lesson. The *Monitor* would no longer employ him as a journalist. His friends turned their backs on him.

Mirebalais withdrew into solitude. He worked at the humblest jobs and quietly pursued what he called "the work of my only friends," composing the books of Kasimir, von Hauptman and Le Gueule, whose sources he diversified—whether out of sheer pride in his craft or because by this stage difficulty had become an antidote to boredom—effecting extraordinary metamorphoses.

In 1994, while visiting a military police sergeant who fondly remembered Mirebalais' society columns and von Hauptman's poems, he just escaped being lynched at the hands of a ragged mob, along with a group of military officers who were preparing to leave the country. Indignant and frightened, Mirebalais retired to Les Cayes, capital of the *Département du sud,* where he rhapsodized in bars and served as a broker on the docks.

Death found him composing the posthumous works of his heteronyms.

# NORTH AMERICAN POETS

# JIM O'BANNON

*Macon 1940–Los Angeles, 1996*

J im O'Bannon, poet and football player, was equally susceptible to the allure of force and a yearning for delicate, perishable things. His earliest literary endeavors are indebted to the Beat esthetic, to judge from his first book of poems, *Macon Night* (1961), published in his hometown, in the short-lived City in Flames series. The texts are preceded by long dedications to Allen Ginsberg, Gregory Corso, Kerouac, Snyder and Ferlinghetti. O'Bannon didn't know these poets personally (at the time he hadn't left his home state of Georgia), but he maintained a profuse and enthusiastic correspondence with at least three of them.

The following year he hitchhiked to New York City, where he met Ginsberg and a black poet at a hotel in the Village. They talked, drank and recited poems. Then Ginsberg and the black guy suggested they make love. At first O'Bannon didn't understand. When one of the poets started to undress him and the other began to stroke him, the terrible truth dawned. For a few seconds he didn't know what to do. Then he punched them away and left. "I would have beaten them to death," he was to say later, "but I felt sorry for them."

In spite of the blows he had received, Ginsberg included four of O'Bannon's poems in a Beat anthology, which was published a year later in New York. O'Bannon, who by that time was back in Georgia, wanted to sue Ginsberg and the publisher. His lawyer advised him against taking legal action. He decided to go back to New York and personally administer the lesson. For days he roamed the city in vain. Later, he would write a poem about the experience: "The Walker," in which an angel crosses New York City on foot without encountering a single righteous man. He also wrote his major poem of estrangement from the Beats, an apocalyptic text that transports the reader to various scenes from history and places in the human soul (the siege of Atlanta by Sherman's troops; the death throes of a Greek shepherd boy; daily life in small towns; caves inhabited by homosexuals, Jews and African Americans; the redeeming sword that hangs over every head, forged from an alloy of gold-colored metals).

In 1963 he traveled to Europe on a Daniel Stone Fellowship for the Development of Young Artists. In Paris he visited Ètienne de Saint-Ètienne, who struck him as dirty and embittered. He also met Jules-Albert Ramis, the great neo-classical French poet and admirer of all things American. It was to be the beginning of a lasting friendship. In a rented car, O'Bannon toured Italy, Yugoslavia and Greece. When the money from the Fellowship ran out, he decided to stay in France. Jules-Albert Ramis found him work at a hotel in

Dieppe which belonged to his family. The hotel turned out to be "more like a cemetery," but the job left O'Bannon plenty of free time for writing. The grey skies over the English Channel gave his inspiration wings. At the end of 1965 an almost unheard-of publisher in Atlanta finally accepted his second book of poetry, the first he felt entirely satisfied with.

But he did not return to the United States. One rainy afternoon, a tourist from Brunswick, Georgia, named Margaret Hogan, came to the hotel. It was love at first sight. Two weeks later, O'Bannon had left his job and was traveling through Spain with the woman who was to be his first wife and his only muse. They were married in a civil ceremony six months later in the French capital; an emotional, melancholic and declamatory Ramis gave the bride away. By then O'Bannon's book had received mixed reviews and prompted a range of comments in the United States' media. Some Beat poets, though not the movement's main figures, reacted in kind to the attacks of the ex-Beat O'Bannon. Others, including Ginsberg, remained indifferent. The book, *The Way of the Brave*, combines a singular vision of nature (a strangely empty nature, devoid of animal life, turbulent and sovereign) with a clear bent for personal insults, defamation and libel, not to mention the threats and bragging that recur, one way or another, in every poem. Some spoke of the "rebirth of a nation," and a few enthusiastic readers believed that they were witnessing the emergence of a new Carl Sandburg for the second half of the twentieth century. Among the poets of Atlanta, however, the book met with a cool and aloof reception.

Meanwhile, in Paris, O'Bannon had joined the Mandarins' Club, a literary group led by Ramis and composed exclusively of his young disciples, two of whom were working on a translation of *The Way of the Brave*, soon to be published under the same imprint as Ramis' own books, a fact that was to play an appreciable role in bolstering O'Bannon's reputation among North American poetry critics, attentive as ever to what was happening across the Atlantic.

In 1970 O'Bannon returned to the States, where each year the bookshop windows displayed a new collection of his poems. *The Way of the Brave* was followed by *Untilled Land, The Burning Stairway of the Poem, Conversation with Jim O'Brady, Apples on the Stairs, The Stairway of Heaven and Hell, New York Revisited, The Best Poems of Jim O'Bannon, The Rivers and Other Poems, The Children of Jim O'Brady in the American Dawn,* and so on.

He made a living giving lectures and readings all around the country. He was married and divorced four times, although he always said that the love of his life was Margaret Hogan. Time mollified his literary invective: there is a yawning gulf between the aggressive sarcasm of "Negative of John Brown" and the Olympian serenity of the ailing poet in "Homage to a Vine Street Dog." He remained firm in his disdain for Jews and homosexuals to the end, although at the time of his death he was beginning, gradually, to accept African Americans.

# RORY LONG

*Pittsburgh, 1952–Laguna Beach, 2017*

ory's father, the poet Marcus Long, was a friend and disciple of Charles Olson, who used to spend a few days each year at the Longs' house in Aserradero, Arizona, near Phoenix (where Marcus was a professor of American literature); a brief, pleasant stay in the company of one of his cherished disciples. So it was in all probability the master himself (and the boy's father, of course) who taught young Rory the right way to read a book of poetry, and gave him his first lessons in projective and non-projective verse. Alternative scenario: hiding under the porch, Rory listened to them talking, while the Arizona dusk settled into eternal fixity.

In any case, to summarize: non-projective verse conforms to traditional versification; it is personal, "closed" poetry, in which it is always possible to detect the self-regard of the citizen-poet, fondling his navel or his balls, complacently displaying his joys or woes; by contrast, projective verse, exemplified on occasion by the work of Ezra Pound and William Carlos Williams, is "open," the poetry of "displaced energy," written according to a technique analogous to "composition by fields." In a word, and to fall into the very same hole as Olson, projective verse is the opposite of non-projective verse.

Or that was how young Rory Long saw it, anyway. "Closed" poetry was Donne and Poe, Robert Browning and Archibald McLeish; "open" poetry was Pound and Williams (but not all of their poems). "Closed" poetry was personal: by the individual poet for the individual reader. "Open" poetry was impersonal: the hunter (the poet) tracking down the memory of his tribe for the recipient and constituent of that memory (the reader). And Rory Long supposed that the Bible was "open" poetry, and that the great multitudes moving or crawling in the shadow of the Book were ideal readers, hungry for the luminous Word. And this enormous, empty edifice was complete in his mind before he reached the age of seventeen. He was energetic then as ever and he set to work immediately. He had to populate and explore the edifice, so the first thing he did was to buy a Bible since he couldn't find one in the house. And then he began to memorize passage after passage, and saw that the poetry spoke directly to his heart.

At twenty he became a preacher in the Church of the True Martyrs of America, and published a book of poetry that no one read, not even his father, who, being a true son of the Enlightenment, was ashamed to see his son crawling with the other crawlers in the shadow of the great Nomadic Book. But no failure could daunt Rory Long, who was already tearing through New Mexico, Arizona, Texas, Oklahoma, Kansas, Colorado, Utah and back to New Mexico, on a whirlwind, counter-clockwise tour. And that was more or less how Rory Long felt: in a whirl, inside out, guts and bones on display; disillusioned with Olson (but not with projective and non-projective verse), whose poems, when he finally read them (which he was slow do to—dazzled by the theory and his own ignorance), seemed almost fraudulent (after reading *The Maximus Poems*, he vomited for three hours); disillusioned with the Church of the True Martyrs of America, whose members could see the plains of the Book but not its centrifugal force, not the volcanoes and underground rivers; disillusioned with the times—the seventies, full of sad hippies and sad whores. He even considered killing himself! But instead he went on reading. And writing: letters, plays, songs, television scripts and movie screenplays, unfinished novels, stories, animal fables, comic-strip plots, biographies, economic and religious pamphlets, and above all poetry, in which he blended all the foregoing genres.

He tried to be impersonal: he wrote visitor's guides to the Book and survival kits for explorers of the Book. He got two tattoos: a broken heart on his right arm, which symbolized his quest, and a book in flames on his left arm, which symbolized his calling. He experimented with oral poetry: not shouting or onomatopoeia, nor the wordplay of the zombies who seem to belong to a tribe parallel to, but different from, the people of the Book; not the whispers of a farmer remembering childhood and sweethearts, but a voice that spoke in warm, familiar tones, like a radio host at the ends of the earth. And he befriended radio hosts, to see if he could learn something from them, like how to recognize the impersonal voice roaming America's radio waves. A tone at once colloquial and dramatic. The voice of the man-who-is-all-eyes wandering around until it finds the consciousness of the man-who-is-all-ears. And so, as the years went by, he moved from church to church and house to house, publishing nothing (unlike his peers), remaining obscure, but writing, submerging himself in the muddy waters of Olson's theory and other theories, weary but open-eyed, worthy son and heir (in spite of himself) to the poet Marcus Long.

When he finally emerged from the underground, he seemed a different man. He was thinner (he measured six foot one and weighed 132 pounds) and older, but he had found the way or at least some short cuts that would soon lead him to the Great Way itself. He had begun preaching for the Texan Church of the Last Days, and his political ideas, which had been muddled in former times, were clear and coherent now. He believed in the necessity of an American resurrection. He believed he *knew* the quite unprecedented characteristics of that resurrection. He believed in the American family: its right to receive the manifold, true message, and its right not to be poisoned by Zionist messages or messages manipulated by the CIA. He believed in individuality and America's need to resume the space race with renewed vigor. He believed that a large part of the Union's body was infected with a mortal disease and that a surgical intervention was required. Having put Olson and his father, but not poetry, behind him (he published a successful collection of short stories, poems and "thoughts" entitled *Noah's Ark*), he devoted himself to spreading his message in the Southwest. And in that he was successful too. The message spread. Via radio waves and video cassettes. It was that simple. And although the past was fading more and more quickly, sometimes he wondered how it could have been so hard to find the true way.

He grew fat (at one point he weighed 265 pounds) and rich, and soon he went where rich people go: California. There he founded the Charismatic Church of Californian Christians. And he had so many followers and it was so easy to spread the Message that he even had time to write sarcastic and humorous poems: texts that made him laugh, and his laughter transformed them into mirrors reflecting his face, unblemished, alone in some Texan room, or with strangers as fat as he was, who called themselves his friends, his biographers, his representatives, at charity dinners within other charity dinners. For example, he wrote a poem in which Leni Riefenstahl makes love with Ernst Jünger. A hundred-year-old man and a ninety-year-old woman. Bones and dead tissue bumping and grinding. God in heaven, said Rory in his big malodorous library, Old Ernst is riding her hard, showing no mercy, and the German whore is crying out for more, more, more. A good poem: the eyes of the elderly pair light up with an enviable brightness; they suck at each other so hard their old jaws creak, while they glance sidelong at the reader, hinting at the lesson. A lesson clear as water. It is time to put an end to democracy. Why are so many Nazis still alive? Take Hess, for example, who would have made it to a hundred if he hadn't committed suicide. What makes them live so long? What makes them almost immortal? The blood they spilled? The flight of the Book? A new level of consciousness? The Charismatic Church of California went underground. A labyrinth where Ernst and Leni went on fucking, unable to uncouple, like a pair of dogs on fire in a valley of sheep. In a valley of blind sheep? A valley of hypnotized sheep? My voice is hypnotizing them, thought Rory Long. But what is the secret of longevity? Purity. Searching, working, preparing for the millennium on various levels. And some nights he felt that he was touching the body of the New Man with the tips of his fingers. He lost a hundred pounds. Ernst and Leni were fucking in the sky for him. And he realized that this was no vulgar, if torrid, hypnotic therapy, but the veritable Host of Fire.

Then he went completely crazy and Cunning occupied every nook of his body. He had money, fame, and good lawyers. He had radio stations, newspapers, magazines, and television networks. And he had robust good health, until one midday in March 2017, when a young African-American man named Baldwin Rocha blew his head off.

# THE ARYAN BROTHERHOOD

Thomas R. Murchison, alias The Texan

*Las Cruces (Texas), 1923–Walla Walla Prison (Oregon), 1979*

Murchison's life was marked from an early age by incarceration. Con-man, car thief, drug dealer and all-round opportunist, he dabbled in a broad range of delinquent activities without developing a particular specialty. It was not ideology that brought him into contact with the Aryan Brotherhood but his repeated prison spells and an implacable will to survive. Given his frail constitution and temperamental aversion to violence, his existence would not have been viable without the support of a group. Although never a leader, he had the honor of establishing the first literary magazine to serve as an organ for the Brotherhood, which he always referred to as "an order for knights of misfortune." The first number of *Literature Behind Bars*, edited by Markus Patterson, Roger Tyler and Thomas R. Murchison, was printed in 1967 at the Crawford penitentiary in Virginia. As well as letters, and news from the prison and Crawford county, the magazine, made up of four tabloid pages, contained some poems (or song lyrics) and three stories. The stories, signed "The Texan," were widely praised: burlesque and fantastic in tone, they portrayed members of the Brotherhood, prisoners or ex-prisoners, fighting the Forces of Evil, in the guise of corrupt politicians or aliens from outer space cunningly disguised as human beings.

The magazine was a success, and in spite of some official opposition set an example for prisoners in other institutions. Murchison's protracted and largely hapless criminal career allowed him to contribute to most of the resulting publications, whether as an active editorial board member, or as a correspondent in another prison.

During his brief periods of freedom, he barely glanced at the newspaper and tried not to associate with ex-prisoners from the Brotherhood. In prison he read Western novels by Zane Grey and others. His favorite writer was Mark Twain. He once wrote that penitentiaries and jail cells had been his Mississippi. He died of pulmonary emphysema. His work, published piecemeal in magazines, consists of more than fifty short stories and a seventy-line poem dedicated to a weasel.

# John Lee Brook

*Napa, California, 1950–Los Angeles, 1997*

Widely regarded as the best writer of the Aryan Brotherhood, and one of the best Californian poets of the late twentieth century, John Lee Brook learned to read and write in the cold classrooms of a prison at the age of eighteen. Up until then his life could be described as a series of misdemeanors without rhyme or reason: normal enough behavior for a poor, white, Californian teenager from a damaged family (father unknown, mother still a kid when she got pregnant, working in poorly paid jobs). Having acquired literacy skills, John Lee Brook became an entirely different kind of criminal: he got into drug dealing, pimping, stealing luxury cars, kidnapping and assassination. In 1990 he was accused of the murder of Jack Brooke and his two bodyguards. At the trial he began by proclaiming his innocence. But surprisingly, ten minutes after climbing into the witness box, he interrupted the attorney, admitted all the charges and declared himself guilty of four unsolved and by then all but forgotten murders. The victims were the pornographer Adolfo Pantoliano, the porn star Suzy Webster, the porn actor Dan Carmine, and the poet Arthur Crane. The first three had been killed four years before the trial; the fourth in 1989. Brook was condemned to death. After various appeals, supported by influential members of the Californian literary community, he was executed in April 1997. According to eye witnesses, he spent his last hours very calmly reading his own poems.

His body of work, which comprises five books, is soundly built; it echoes Whitman, makes abundant use of colloquialisms, and has strong affinities with the new narrative poetry, while remaining open to other North American schools and trends. His favorite themes, which recur with a sometimes obsessive frequency throughout his work, are the extreme poverty of certain sectors of the white population, African Americans and sexual abuse in the prison system, Mexicans (always portrayed as diminutive devils or mysterious cooks), the absence of women, motorcycle clubs considered the inheritors of the frontier spirit, gangster hierarchies on the streets and in prison, the decadence of America, and solitary warriors.

The following poems merit special attention:

—"Vindication of John L. Brook," the first of a series of torrential texts, all more than 500 lines long, which the author used to describe as "broken novels." In the "Vindication" Brook is already fully formed as a poet, although he was only twenty when he wrote it. The poem is about the diseases of youth, and the only proper way to cure them.

—"Street without a Name," a text in which quotations

from MacLeish and Conrad Aiken are combined with the menus of the Orange County jail and the pederastic dreams of a literature professor who taught classes for the prisoners on Tuesdays and Thursdays.

—"Santino and Me," fragments of conversations between the poet and his parole officer, Lou Santino, relating to sports (which is the most American sport?), whores, the lives of movie stars, and prison celebrities and their moral authority both inside and outside.

—"Charlie" (one such prison celebrity), a brief and "concrete" but nonetheless affectionate portrait of Charles Manson, whom the author met, it seems, in 1992.

—"Lady Companions," an epiphany featuring psychopaths, serial killers, various mentally deranged individuals, bipolar sufferers obsessed with the American dream, sleepwalkers and stealthy hunters.

—"The Bad," an insight into the world of natural born killers, portrayed by Brook as "Ignoble beings   children possessed by will   in an iron labyrinth or desert   Vulnerable as pigs in a cage full of lionesses . . ."

This final poem, dated 1985 and published in his third book of poetry (*Solitude*, 1986), was the subject of two controversial studies in the *Southern California Journal of Psychology* and the *Berkeley Psychology Magazine*.

# THE FABULOUS
# SCHIAFFINO BOYS

## ITALO SCHIAFFINO

*Buenos Aires, 1948–Buenos Aires, 1982*

It is probably true to say that no poet has ever been more diligent than Italo Schiaffino, not among his contemporaries in Buenos Aires at any rate, in spite of which was he was eventually overshadowed by the growing reputation of his younger brother, Argentino Schiaffino, also a poet.

The boys came from a humble family, and there were only two passions in Italo's life: soccer and literature. At fifteen, two years after leaving school to work as an errand boy in Don Ercole Massantonio's hardware store, he joined Enzo Raúl Castiglione's gang, one of the many groups of Boca Juniors hooligans that existed at the time.

He soon made headway. In 1968, when Castiglione was imprisoned, Italo Schiaffino took over the leadership of the group and wrote his first poem (his first recorded poem, in any case) and his first manifesto. Entitled *Cower, Hounds!,* the poem is 300 lines long, and his friends from the gang could recite the highlights by heart. Basically, it is a war poem; in the words of Schiaffino, "a kind of *Iliad* for the Boca boys." A thousand copies were printed in 1969 with money raised by subscription. The edition contained a preface by Dr. Pérez Heredia in which he welcomed the new poet to the Argentinean Parnassus. The manifesto was a different matter. In five pages, Schiaffino outlined the situation of soccer in Argentina, lamented the crisis, identified the guilty parties (the Jewish plutocracy, which hadn't produced a single good player, and the Red intelligentsia, responsible for the nation's decadence). He indicated the danger and explained the ways to exorcize it. The manifesto was called *The Time of Argentinean Youth*, and in the words of Schiaffino it was "a kind of Latin American version of von Clausewitz, a wake-up call to the nation's inquiring minds." It soon became obligatory reading among the hard-line members of Castiglione's old gang.

In 1971, Schiaffino visited the widow Mendiluce, but there are no records, photographic or written, of their meeting. In 1972, he published *The Path to Glory*, a series of forty-five poems, each one examining the life of a different Boca Juniors player. Like *Cower, Hounds!* the book included an obliging preface by Dr. Pérez Heredia and a *nihil obstat* issued by the vice-president of the soccer club. The publication was financed by the members of Schiaffino's gang, who paid a subscription, and the remaining copies were sold in the vicinity of Boca's Bombonera stadium on match days. This time the sportswriters paid him some attention: two magazines deemed *The Path to Glory* worthy of a review, and when Dr. Pestalozzi's radio program *100% Soccer* organized a round table on the critical state of the national game, Schiaffino was invited to participate. On the radio, in the company of well-known sports personalities, he was restrained.

In 1975 he delivered his next collection of poetry to the printer. Entitled *Like Wild Bulls*, it has a gaucho-like tone, which can reasonably be attributed to the influence of Hernández, Giraldes and Carriego. In it, Schiaffino recounts, sometimes in great detail, how he led the gang on excursions to various places in the province of Buenos Aires, as well as on two trips to Córdoba and Rosario, which resulted in victories for the visiting team and their hoarse supporters as well as sundry skirmishes, none of which degenerated into street battles, although a number of lessons were administered to isolated elements of the "enemy forces." In spite of its eminently bellicose tone, *Like Wild Bulls* is Schiaffino's most successful work. Exhibiting a degree of freedom and spontaneity unmatched elsewhere in his writing, it gives the reader a clear sense of the young poet's character and his bond with "the virginal spaces of the Fatherland."

In 1975, after the fusion of his gang with those of Honesto García and Juan Carlos Lentini, Schiaffino launched the triennial magazine *With Boca*, which thenceforth was to serve as a mouthpiece for the expression and diffusion of his ideas. In the first number of 1976, he published "Jews Out": out of the soccer stadiums naturally, not out of Argentina, but the essay was widely misunderstood and earned him many enemies. As did "Memoirs of a Malcontent Fan," published in the third number of 1976, in which Schiaffino, pretending to be a River Plate fan, pokes fun at the players and supporters of Boca's traditional rival. Parts II, III and IV of the "Memoirs" followed in the first and third numbers of 1977 and the first number of 1978. Unanimously acclaimed by the readers of *With Boca*, they were quoted by Colonel (retired) Persio de la Fuente in an article on the idiom of the Latin American picaresque in the *University of Buenos Aires Semiotics Review*.

1978 was Schiaffino's year of glory. Argentina won the World Cup for the first time and the gang celebrated in the streets, which were transformed for the occasion into a vast parade ground. It was the year of "A Toast to the Boys," an excessive, allegorical poem, in which Schiaffino imagines a country setting forth to meet its destiny, united like one huge soccer gang. It was also the year in which "respectable," "adult" avenues opened up for him: his poem was widely reviewed, and not just in sports magazines. A Buenos Aires radio station offered him a job as a commentator; a newspaper with close links to the government offered him a weekly column on youth issues. Schiaffino accepted all the offers but before long his impetuous pen had alienated everyone. At the radio station and the newspaper it soon became clear that leading the Boca boys was more important to Schiaffino than being on any payroll. Broken ribs and windows resulted from the conflict, and the first of a long series of prison terms.

Without the support of his benefactors, Schiaffino's lyric inspiration seems to have dried up. From 1978 to 1982, he devoted himself almost exclusively to the gang and to bringing out *With Boca*, in which he continued to rail against the ills besetting soccer and Argentina.

His authority over the fan base remained undiminished. Under his leadership the Boca gang grew in numbers and strength as never before. His prestige, albeit obscure and secret, was unrivalled: the family album still contains photos of Schiaffino with players and club officials.

He died of a heart attack in 1982, while listening to one of the last reports on the Falklands War.

# Argentino ("Fatso") Schiaffino

### *Buenos Aires, 1956–Detroit, 2015*

The arc of Argentino Schiaffino's life has prompted comparisons, over the years, with varied and often incompatible figures from the worlds of literature and sports. Thus, in 1978, a certain Palito Kruger, writing in the third number of *With Boca*, asserted that Schiaffino's life and work were comparable to those of Rimbaud. In 1982, in a different number of the same magazine, Argentino Schiaffino was referred to as the Latin American equivalent of Dionisio Ridruejo. In the preface to his 1995 anthology *Occult Poets of Argentina*, Professor González Irujo put him on a par with Baldomero Fernández, and with his own personal friends. Letters to Buenos Aires newspapers hailed him as the only civic figure in the same league as Maradona. And in 2015, a short death notice written by John Castellano for a newspaper in Selma (Alabama) coupled him with the tragic figure of Ringo Bonavena.

All the comparisons are justified, to a certain degree, by the ups and downs of Argentino Schiaffino's life and work.

We know that he grew up in the shadow of his brother, who taught him to love soccer, recruited him as a Boca fan, and interested him in the mysteries of poetry. The two brothers were, however, notably different. Italo Schiaffino was tall, well built, authoritarian, unemotional and unimaginative. He cut an imposing figure: wiry, angular, with a slightly cadaverous air, although from the age of twenty-eight, perhaps because of a hormonal imbalance, he began to grow dangerously fat, eventually reaching a fatal degree of obesity. Argentino Schiaffino was on the shorter side of average, plump (thence the affectionate nickname "Fatso," by which he was known until the day he died), sociable and bold by nature, charismatic though hardly authoritarian.

He began to write poetry at the age of thirteen. At sixteen, while his elder brother was making his name with *The Path to Glory*, he produced fifty mimeographed copies of his first book, at his own expense and risk. It was a series of thirty epigrams entitled *Anthology of the Best Argentinean Jokes*; over one weekend he personally sold all the copies to members of the Boca gangs. In April 1973, employing the same editorial strategy, he published his story "The Invasion of Chile," an exercise in black humor (some passages resemble a splatter movie script) about a hypothetical war between the two republics. In December of the same year he published the manifesto *We're Not Going to Take It*, in which he attacked the league's umpires, whom he accused of bias, lack of physical fitness, and, in some cases, of drug use.

He began the year 1974 by publishing the collection *Iron Youth* (fifty mimeographed copies): dense, militaristic poems with marching-song rhythms, which, if nothing else, obliged Schiaffino to venture beyond the bounds of his natural thematic domains: soccer and humor. He followed up with a play, *The Presidential Summit, or What Can We Do to Turn This Around?* In this five-act farce, heads of state and diplomats from various Latin American nations meet in a hotel room somewhere in Germany to discuss options for restoring the natural and traditional supremacy of Latin American soccer, which is under threat from the European total-football approach. The play, which is extremely long, recalls a certain strain of avant-garde theater, from Adamov, Genet and Grotowski to Copi and Savary, although it is unlikely (though not impossible) that Fatso ever set foot in the sort of establishment given to the production of such plays. The following are only a few of the scenes: 1. A monologue about the etymology of the words "peace" and "art" delivered by the Venezuelan cultural attaché. 2. The rape of the Nicaraguan ambassador in one of the hotel bathrooms by the presidents of Nicaragua, Colombia and Haiti. 3. A tango danced by the presidents of Argentina and Chile. 4. The Uruguayan ambassador's peculiar interpretation of the prophecies of Nostradamus. 5. A masturbation contest organized by the presidents, with three categories: thickness (won by the Ecuadorian ambassador); length (won by the Brazilian ambassador); and, most importantly, distance covered by semen (won by the Argentinean ambassador). 6. The president of Costa Rica's subsequent irritation and condemnation of such contests as "scatology in the poorest taste." 7. The arrival of the German whores. 8. Mass brawling, chaos and exhaustion. 9. The arrival of the dawn, a "pink dawn that intensifies the fatigue of the bigwigs who finally come to understand their defeat." 10. The president of

Argentina's solitary breakfast, after which he lets off a series of resounding farts, then climbs into bed and falls asleep.

In the same year, 1974, Argentino Schiaffino managed to publish two more works. A short manifesto in *With Boca*, entitled "Satisfactory Solutions," which is, in a sense, a sequel to *The Presidential Summit* (Latin America should respond to total football, he suggests, by physically eliminating its finest exponents, that is to say, assassinating Cruyf, Beckenbauer, et cetera). And a new collection of poems (a hundred mimeographed copies): *Spectacle in the Sky*, a series of short, light—one might almost say winged—poems about the stars of Boca Juniors down through the years, not unlike Italo Schiaffino's famous book *The Path to Glory*. The theme is the same, the technique is similar, some metaphors are identical, yet where the elder brother's work is ruled by rigor and the determination to record a history of striving, the younger brother yields to the pleasure of discovering images and rhymes, treats the old legends humorously but not without affection, applies a light touch where Italo was grave, and mounts a powerful and occasionally opulent verbal display. This book probably contains the best of Argentino Schiaffino's work.

Some years of literary silence followed. In 1975 he got married and started working in an auto repair shop. After which he is said to have hitch-hiked to Patagonia, read everything he could lay his hands on, submerged himself in the study of the history of the Americas, and experimented with psychotropic drugs, but what we know for certain is that he was there with his brother's gang every week, whether the game was at home or away, cheering with the best of them. During this period he is also said to have participated in the activities of Captain Antonio Lacouture's death squad, driving and repairing a small fleet of cars kept at a villa on the outskirts of Buenos Aires, but of this there is no proof.

During the 1978 World Cup, which was hosted by Argentina, Fatso resurfaced with a long poem entitled *Champions* (1,000 mimeographed copies, which he sold himself at the stadium's entrances and exits): a rather difficult and occasionally muddled text, which jumps abruptly from free verse to alexandrines, to distichs, to rhyming couplets and sometimes even to catalectics (when exploring the ins and outs of the Argentinean selection it adopts the tone of Lorca's *Romancero gitano*, and when examining the rival teams it veers between the devious advice of old Vizcacha in *Martin Fierro* and Manrique's straightforward predictions in the "Coplas"). The book sold out in two weeks.

Then there was another long period of literary silence. In 1982, as he was to reveal in his autobiography, he tried to enlist as a volunteer to fight the British in the Falklands. He was unsuccessful. Shortly afterward, he traveled to Spain for the World Cup with a group of die-hard fans. After the defeat of the Argentinean team by Italy, he was arrested in a Barcelona hotel, on charges of assault, attempted homicide, robbery and disorderly conduct. He spent three months in Barcelona's Model Prison along with five other Argentinean soccer fans, before being released for want of evidence. On his return, the Boca gang hailed him as their new leader, but uninspired by this promotion he generously delegated the role to Dr. Morazán and the contractor Scotti Cabello. Nevertheless, his moral authority over the followers of his late brother would remain undiminished to the end of his life, a life that for many of the younger fans had begun to take on the aura of legend.

*With Boca* folded in 1983, despite the best efforts of Dr. Morazán, thus depriving Fatso of his sole means of public expression; the deprivation, however, would prove beneficial in the long term. In 1984, a small politico-literary publisher, Black & White, brought out a volume entitled *Impenitent Memoirs*, Argentino Schiaffino's first venture beyond the realm of self-publication, which was greeted with indifference by the literary set. It is a small volume of stories in a decidedly naturalistic mode. In less than four pages, the longest story evokes mornings and evenings spent playing soccer in a working-class neighborhood of Buenos Aires. The characters are four children who call themselves the Four Gauchos of the Apocalypse, and a number of hagiographers have taken their experiences to reflect the childhood of the Schiaffino brothers. The shortest story occupies less than half a page: jocular in tone and larded with Buenos Aires slang, it describes a sickness or a heart attack or perhaps simply a bout of melancholy afflicting some nameless, distant person in the course of an ordinary afternoon.

In 1985, the collection of stories *Crazy Blunders* appeared under the same imprint. At only 56 pages, it was even slimmer than its predecessor, to which, at first glance, it appeared to be an epilogue. This book did, however, attract some critical attention. One review summarily dispatched it as cretinous. One tore it to shreds, but without impugning Schiaffino's feel for language. Two other reviewers (there were only four in all) were forthright and more or less enthusiastic in their praise.

Black & White went bankrupt soon afterwards, and Schiaffino seems to have lapsed not only into silence, as on previous occasions, but also into anonymity. It was suggested that his disappearance could be explained by the fact that he owned half or at least a significant proportion of the shares in Black & White. How Schiaffino got hold of enough money to have a substantial stake in a publishing company remains a mystery. There was some talk of funds obtained during the dictatorship, wealth stolen and secreted, undisclosed sources of income, but nothing could be proved.

In 1987 Argentino Schiaffino reappeared at the helm of the Boca gang. He had separated from his wife and was working as a waiter in a downtown restaurant on Corrientes, where his proverbial good humor soon made him one of the neighborhood's favorite characters. At the end of the year he published three stories, none of which exceeded seven pages, in a mimeographed collection entitled *The Great Buenos Aires Restaurant Novel*, which he sold without compunction to his clients. The first story is about a Lebanese who arrives in Buenos Aires and looks for a solid business in which to invest his savings. He falls in love with an Argentinean woman who works as a butcher, and together they decide to open a restaurant specializing in meat of all kinds. Everything goes well until the Lebanese man's poor relatives start turning up. In the end the butcher solves the problem by liquidating the relatives one by one, with the help of her kitchen hand and lover, nicknamed Monkey. The story ends with an apparently bucolic scene: the butcher, her husband and Monkey set off to spend a day in the country and prepare a barbecue under the wide open skies of the Fatherland. The second story is about an old magnate in the Buenos Aires restaurant business who wants to find his last love, and with that objective scours nightclubs, brothels, the houses of friends with grown-up daughters, et cetera. He finally discovers the woman of his dreams in his first restaurant: a twenty-year-old tango singer, blind since birth. The third story is about a group of friends dining in a restaurant which belongs to one of them and has been closed to the public for the evening. At first the occasion seems to be a stag night, then a celebration of something one of the friends has achieved, then a wake, then a gastronomical gathering with no other purpose than to enjoy good Argentinean cooking, and finally appears to be a trap set for a traitor by all or almost all the others, although, beyond vague mentions of trust, eternal friendship, loyalty and honor, we never learn what the supposed traitor has betrayed. The story is ambiguous and based entirely on the conversation of the diners at the table, whose number declines as the evening wears on, while their words become increasingly pompous and cruel, or, on the contrary, clipped, laconic and sharp. Regrettably, the story comes to a predictable, not to say gratuitously violent, end: the traitor is hacked to pieces in the restaurant bathroom.

Nineteen eighty-seven was also the year in which Schiaffino's long poem "Solitude" (640 lines) was published at the expense of Dr. Morazán, who penned a preface illustrated by his niece Miss Bertha Macchio Morazán with four India-ink drawings. *Solitude* is an odd, desperate, turbulent text, which casts some light on obscure stretches of its author's biography. The events take place during the 1986 World Cup, both in the host nation, Mexico, and in Argentina. Schiaffino, who is the poem's unrivaled protagonist, reflects on the "solitude of the champions" in a seedy, out-of-the-way hotel in Buenos Aires, which sometimes seems to be an abandoned ranch far out on the vast pampas. Then we see him flying to Mexico on Aerolineas Argentinas, accompanied by "two black guards," members of his gang, perhaps, or threatening figures. His time in Mexico is largely divided between bars of the most disreputable variety, where he is able to verify *in situ* the devastating effects of miscegenation (although he generally gets on well with "Mexican drunks," who see in him a "snail prince, master of a ruined tower") and the provincial boarding houses where he finds lodging as he follows the movements of the boys in blue and white. The final victory of the Argentinean team is an apotheosis: Schiaffino sees an enormous light hovering over Aztec stadium like a flying saucer and transparent figures emerging from the light, accompanied by little dogs with human faces and flaming fur, restrained on metallic leashes by the transparent beings. He also sees a finger, "roughly thirty yards long," perhaps ominously pointing the way, perhaps simply indicating a cloud in the vast sky. The party continues in the "flood-locked" streets of the Mexican capital, and ends with an exhausted Fatso returning to the solitude of his boarding-house room and passing out.

In 1988, having adopted photocopying, he published a story entitled "The Ostrich" in an edition of fifty booklets. It is, at least in principle, a homage to the soldiers of the military coup, yet in spite of the Schiaffino's evident admiration for order, the family and the Fatherland, he was unable to refrain from sallies of caustic, cruel, scatologically humorous sallies, intemperate, caricatural, parodic, irreverent outbursts—the Schiaffino trademark in short. The following year *The Best of Argentino Schiaffino* appeared, without a publisher's imprint or date: a selection of his poems, stories and political writings. The cognoscenti were quick to surmise that the book had been produced by The Fourth Reich in Argentina, a mystagogically inspired venture, which kept popping up and then vanishing again in Buenos Aires publishing between 1965 and 2000.

Gradually Schiaffino began to acquire something of a

media profile. He took part in a television program on soccer gangs, and was the first to defend their right to violence, on grounds such as honor, self-defense, group solidarity, and the pure and simple pleasure of street fighting. Invited as a defendant, he assumed the role of prosecutor. He participated in radio and television debates on all sorts of subjects: fiscal policy, the decadence of the young Latin American democracies, the future of the tango on the European music scene, the state of opera in Buenos Aires, the exorbitant prices of couture fashion, public education in the provinces, widespread ignorance about the nation's extent and borders, Argentinean wine, the privatization of the country's leading industries, the Formula One Grand Prix, tennis and chess, the work of Borges, Bioy Casares, Cortázar and Mújica Lainez (about whose work he made bold pronouncements, although he swore he had never read it), the life of Roberto Arlt (for whom he professed his admiration, although the novelist had "belonged to the enemy camp"), border incidents, how to end unemployment, white-collar crime and street crime, the inventiveness of the Argentineans, the sawmills of the Andes, and the works of Shakespeare.

He attended the 1990 World Cup in Italy, one of a group of thirty Argentinean fans classified as potentially dangerous aliens. Prior to the trip he had expressed a wish to meet with the British hooligans for a reconciliation ceremony consisting of a mass for the casualties of the Falklands War, followed by a barbecue. Although it was never anything more than a wish, the news spread around the world, and by the time he returned to Argentina, Schiaffino's renown had increased considerably.

In 1991 he brought out two books: *Chimichurri Sauce*

(self-published, forty pages, 100 copies), an unfortunate imitation of Lugones and Darío, lapsing occasionally into pure plagiarism, which left all but a few readers wondering why he had written and, having written, *published* it; and *The Iron Boat* (La Castaña, 50 pages, 500 copies), a series of thirty prose poems whose central theme is the phenomenon of friendship between men. The book's trite message, that friendship is forged in danger, seems in retrospect to foreshadow the life that Fatso was to lead in the coming years. In 1992, commanding a substantial group recruited from his gang, he orchestrated the ambush on a public highway of a bus carrying River Plate supporters, resulting in two deaths from gunshot wounds and numerous injuries. A warrant for his arrest was issued; Argentino Schiaffino disappeared. In phone calls to various radio stations he vigorously declared his innocence, although he did not condemn the ambush—on the contrary—and several witnesses, including more than one ex-member of Schiaffino's gang, said they had seen him near the scene of the crime. In the media he was soon identified as the mastermind and instigator of the incident. Here begins the shadowy phase of his life, especially propitious to all kinds of speculation and mystification.

While on the run, he is known to have attended soccer matches: photos he set up himself showed him rooting for the team like any other fan. The gang, the inner circle of the gang, those who had stood by the Schiaffino boys from the start, protected him with a fanatical devotion. His life on the run inspired awe among the youngsters. A few read his works; some imitated him and tried to follow his literary lead, but Fatso was inimitable.

In 1994, when the World Cup was being played in the

United States, Fatso gave an interview to a Buenos Aires sports magazine. Where was he? In Boston. A major scandal broke out. The Argentinean sportswriters became suspicious after being subjected to special security measures—slights, so they felt, to their professional dignity—and commented sarcastically about the North American police procedures. The other Latin American journalists, plus a few from Spain, Italy and Portugal, echoed their mockery. The story, just one of the many generated by the event, was repeated around the world. The Boston police and the FBI swung into action, but Schiaffino had disappeared.

For a long time, his whereabouts were entirely unknown. The gang even publicly admitted to being in the dark, until Scotti Cabello, who was in prison, received a long poem entitled "Terra autem erat inanis" in a letter from Fatso, postmarked Orlando, Florida. The epistle, which Dr. Morazán hastened to publish, obliging the Boca fans to pay a subscription, begins with a comparison, in rhythmic free verse, of the open spaces of North America and those of Argentina, at opposite extremes of the continent, continues with detailed reminiscences of the prisons that "the author and his friends" have come to know through their "enthusiasm and innocence" (a clear allusion to the two-year sentence that Scotti Cabello was serving at the time) and ends in a chaotic blend of threats and idyllic visions of a childhood paradise regained (mamma, the smell of fresh pasta, brothers laughing around the table, playing soccer in vacant lots with a plastic ball until nightfall) and irreverent, off-color jokes, a characteristic trait of Schiaffino's late manner.

There was no further news of him until 1999. The gang observed an absolute and perhaps ingenuous silence. In spite of Dr. Morazan's insinuations—his deliberately enigmatic utterances and ambiguities—it is probably the case that no one in Argentina had any idea what had become of Fatso. It was all speculation. Even so, in 1998 the die-hard fans set off to France for the World Cup, convinced that they would find him cheering on the boys in blue and white, as always. But they were entirely mistaken. Fatso had turned away from the first of his two great loves and devoted himself to the second: he read everything he could lay his hands on, especially history books, crime novels and best-sellers; learned English to a rudimentary level (which he would never surpass); and married a North American, María Teresa Greco, from New Jersey, twenty years his senior, thereby obtaining US citizenship. He was living in Beresford, a small town in southern Florida, working as chief barman in a restaurant owned by a Cuban, and unhurriedly concocting what was to be his first novel, a five-hundred page thriller set in various countries over several years. His habits had changed. He had become orderly, and was leading an almost monk-like existence.

In 1999, as mentioned above, he reemerged. Scotti Cabello, who was out of prison and had more or less withdrawn from the turbulent world of the soccer gangs, received not a letter but a telephone call from Fatso. He was flabbergasted. Fatso's voice, sounding just the same as ever, reeled off plans, projects and strategies for revenge, with the undiminished enthusiasm of his early years, giving Scotti the disturbing impression that, for his old hero, time had stopped. Fatso didn't seem perturbed by the news that he was no longer the leader of the Boca gang. He had instructions still, and hoped that Scotti would carry them out. First, let the boys know that he was alive; second, trumpet the news that he was coming home; third, start looking for someone to publish his great North American novel in Spanish . . .

Scotti Cabello loyally satisfied the first two demands, but could find no takers in Argentina for Fatso's literary opus. In the end it was Schiaffino who failed to fulfill his promise: after raising hopes of his return—if only among a few followers—he lapsed once again into sullen silence.

During the 2002 World Cup in Japan, a few Argentinean supporters scanning the Osaka stadium with binoculars thought they saw him in a side row, near the south end. They made their way towards the spot, uncertain and excited, but when they got there, he had gone. Three years later the Bucaneros publishing house in Tampa brought out his *Memoirs of an Argentinean* (350 pages), a book full of gangsters, car chases, gorgeous women, unsolved murders, bars where private eyes meet with honest cops, adventures in the ghetto, corrupt politicians, movie stars receiving threats, voodoo rituals, industrial espionage, etc. The book was relatively successful, at least among the Hispanic community in Miami and in the U.S. Southwest.

By then Schiaffino had been widowed and married again. According to some sources, he had links with the Ku Klux Klan, the American Christian Movement and the Rebirth of America group. But in fact he was dividing his time between business and literature. He owned two barbeque restaurants in the Miami area, and was immersed in the elaboration of a major work in progress, which he was keeping strictly under wraps.

In 2007 he self-published a book of prose poems, *The Horsemen of Repentance*, in which he relates, although in a muddled or deliberately hermetic manner, some of his adventures in North America, from his arrival as a wanted man up to the moment when he met Elisabeth Moreno, his third wife, to whom the book is dedicated.

Finally, in 2010, the long-promised, long-awaited novel appeared. Its title was laconic and suggestive: *The Treasure*. The plot is a thin disguise for a memoir in which Argentino Schiaffino discusses and analyses his life, taking it apart, weighing good and bad, seeking and finding justifications. In the course of the book's 535 pages, the reader is made privy to undisclosed aspects of the author's existence, some of which are genuinely surprising, although as a rule Schiaffino's revelations are restricted to the domestic sphere: we learn, for example, that since they were unable to have children of their own, he and Elisabeth adopted a six-year-old Irish boy named Tommy, and a four-year-old Mexican girl named Cynthia, whom they renamed Cynthia-Elisabeth, in accordance with Fatso's wish, etc. Schiaffino makes his political position clear. From his own point of view, at least. He is neither on the right nor on the left. He has black friends and friends in the Ku Klux Klan (among the photos in the book, one shows a barbecue in a back yard; all the guests are wearing Klan hoods and gowns, except for Schiaffino, who is in chef's garb, using a spare white hood to wipe the sweat from his neck). He is against monopolies, especially cultural monopolies. He believes in the family, but also in a man's "natural right to have a bit of fun on the side." He trusts in the United States, of which he has become a citizen, while drawing up a long list of trivial things that ought to be improved.

The chapters devoted to his life in Argentina, and especially to his leading role in the soccer gangs, are sketchy compared to those about his experiences in North America. The book contains historical inaccuracies, which may, however, be deranged metaphors for truths of another kind. For example, he says that he took part in the Falklands War as a private, was awarded the San Martín Medal for his bravery in various engagements, and promoted to Sergeant. His description of the battle of Goose Green is full of blackly humorous details but is not always believable from a strictly military point of view. He says almost nothing of his long career as the head of the Boca fans. He does, however, complain that in Argentina his books were never given much attention. On the other hand, his life in the United States, both real and imaginary, is recounted with zest and in minute detail. Many chapters of the book are devoted to women, among whom a place of honor is reserved for his second wife, the "beloved and sorely missed companion" who opened the doors of "her personal library" to him. As to sports, he is interested only in boxing, and the characters who haunt the boxing world provide him with a wealth of material: Italians, Cubans, melancholic old black men, friends and tireless storytellers one and all.

After the publication of *The Treasure*, Schiaffino seemed to have settled down for good. But it was not to be. Bad management or bad friends bankrupted him. He lost his two restaurants. Divorce was not long in coming. In 2013 he left Florida and moved to New Orleans, where he worked as the manager of a restaurant called El Chacarero Argentino. At the end of that year, he self-published his last book of poems: *A Story Heard in the Delta*, a collection of melancholic but nonetheless outrageous jokes, in the vein of the best verse from his Boca period. In 2015, he left New Orleans for reasons that have not been ascertained, and a few months later an unidentified individual or individuals killed him in the backyard of a gambling den in Detroit.

# THE INFAMOUS
# RAMÍREZ HOFFMAN

# Carlos Ramírez Hoffman

*Santiago de Chile, 1950–Lloret de Mar, Spain, 1998*

The infamous Ramírez Hoffman must have launched his career in 1970 or 1971, when Salvador Allende was president of Chile.

He almost certainly attended the writing workshop run by Juan Cherniakovski in the southern city of Concepción. At that stage he was calling himself Emilio Stevens and writing poems of which Cherniakovski did not disapprove, although the stars of the workshop were the twins María and Magdalena Venegas, seventeen- or perhaps eighteen-year-old poets from Nacimiento, who were studying sociology and psychology respectively.

Emilio Stevens was going steady (an expression that gives me goose bumps now) with María Venegas, although in fact he often went out with both sisters, to the movies, concerts, plays or lectures, that sort of thing; sometimes they went to the beach in the girls' car, a white Volkswagon Beetle, to watch the sun sink into the Pacific and smoke some dope. I suppose the Venegas girls went out with other guys, and Stevens probably had other friends too; at the time, we all thought we knew what there was to know about each other's lives, a fairly stupid assumption, as events were soon to demonstrate. Why did the Venegas sisters get mixed up with him? It's a trivial mystery, an everyday accident. The man known as Stevens was, I suppose, handsome, intelligent, sensitive.

A week after the coup, in September 1973, in the midst of the reigning confusion, the Venegas sisters left their apartment in Concepción and went back home to Nacimiento. That was where they lived with their aunt. Their parents, both painters, had died before the girls turned fifteen, leaving them the house and some land in the province of Bio-Bio, which provided a comfortable living. The sisters would often speak of them, and their poems often featured imaginary painters lost in the wilds of southern Chile, embarking on hopelessly ambitious works and hopelessly in love. Once, and once only, I had the opportunity to examine a photo of them: the father was dark and thin, with a certain look of sadness and perplexity peculiar to those born on this side of the river Bío-Bío; the mother was taller, slightly chubby, with a sweet, easy-going smile.

They went to Nacimiento and shut themselves up in their house, one of the biggest houses in town, on the outskirts, a two-storey wooden house that had belonged to the father's family, with more than seven rooms, and a piano, and the powerful presence of the aunt, who kept the twins safe from all harm, although they were not what you would call faint-hearted girls, quite the opposite.

And one fine day, say two weeks or a month later, Emilio Stevens turned up in Nacimiento. It must have happened something like this. One night, or perhaps it was earlier, one afternoon, one of those melancholic southern afternoons, in mid-spring, someone knocks at the door, and it is Emilio Stevens. The Venegas girls are pleased to see him; they bombard him with questions, invite him to dinner and then say he's welcome to stay the night; and after dinner they probably read out poems, not Stevens, he doesn't want to read anything, he says is working on something new, smiles in a mysterious, knowing way, or perhaps he doesn't even smile, just flatly says no, and the Venegas girls approve; in their innocence, they think they understand, but they don't understand at all, and yet they think they understand, and they read their poems, which are dense and very good: a blend of Violeta and Nicanor Parra and Enrique Lihn, if such a thing is conceivable, a mind-blowing distillation of Joyce Mansour, Sylvia Plath and Alejandra Pizarnik, the ideal cocktail with which to bid the day farewell, a day in 1973, fading irretrievably. And during the night Emilio Stevens gets up like a sleepwalker, perhaps he has slept with María Venegas, perhaps not, at any rate he gets up without hesitation, like a sleepwalker, and goes to the aunt's room, hearing the motor of a car approaching the house, and then he cuts the aunt's throat, no, he stabs her in the heart, it's cleaner, quicker; he covers her mouth and plunges the knife into her heart, then he goes down and opens the door, and two men come into the house that belongs to the stars of Juan Cherniakovski's poetry workshop, and the fucked-up night comes into the house and then it goes out again, almost straight away, the night comes in, and out it goes, swift and efficient.

And the bodies vanish, but no, years later one will appear in a mass grave, that of Magdalena Venegas, but only hers, as if to prove that Ramírez Hoffman is a man and not a god. Many other people disappeared at that time, like Juan Cherniakovski, the Jewish poet of the South, and no one was surprised that he had disappeared, the Red son of a bitch, although later, following in the footsteps of his putative Russian-Jewish uncle, he turned up in all the trouble spots of Latin America, becoming a legend, the model of the itinerant Chilean: there he was in Nicaragua, El Salvador, Guatemala, with his rifle and his fist in the air, as if to say Here I am, you bastards, the last Jewish Bolshevik from the forests of southern Chile, until one day he disappeared for good, possibly killed during the FMLN's final offensive. And Concepción's other poet, Martín García, Cherniakovski's friend and rival, who held his workshop in the medical faculty, also disappeared. The two of them were always together, talking about poetry. If the sky over Chile had begun to crumble and fall, they would have gone on talking about poetry: the tall, fair-haired Cherniakovski and the short, dark Martín García; Cherniakovski mainly interested in Latin American poetry, while García was translating French poets no one else had heard of. This of course infuriated a lot of people. How could that ugly little Indian presume to translate and correspond with Alain Jouffroy, Denis Roche, and Marcelin Pleynet? Michel Bulteau, Matthieu Messagier, Claude Pelieu, Franck Venaille, Pierre Tilman, Daniel Biga . . . who *were* these people, for God's sake? And what was so special about this Georges Perec character, published by Denoîl, whose books García was always toting around, pretentious bastard. Nobody missed him. Many would have been glad to hear of his death. Writing this now it seems hard to believe. But García reappeared in exile, like Cherniakovski (whom he no doubt never saw again), first in East Germany, which he left as soon as he could, then in France, where he scraped together a living teaching Spanish and translating for small presses, mainly books by offbeat, early twentieth-century Latin American writers obsessed with mathematical or pornographic quandaries. Later on Martín García was killed too, but that is an entirely different story.

Following the coup, as the flimsy power structure of the Popular Unity government was being torn down, I was taken prisoner. The circumstances of my arrest were banal if not grotesque, but as a result I was able to witness Ramírez Hoffman's first poetic act, although at that stage I didn't know who Ramírez Hoffman was or what had befallen the Venegas sisters.

It happened late one afternoon—Ramírez Hoffman was fond of twilight—while I was killing time along with the rest of the prisoners at the La Peña detention center, on the outskirts of Concepción, practically in Talcahuano, playing chess in the yard of our makeshift prison. A few strands of cloud appeared in the sky, which had been absolutely clear. The clouds, shaped like cigarettes or pencils, were black and white at first, then pink, and finally bright vermillion. I think I was the only prisoner looking at them. Then, among the clouds, the airplane appeared. An old airplane. At first a spot no bigger than a mosquito. Silent. It was coming from over the sea and gradually approaching Concepción. Heading for the city center. It seemed to be moving as slowly as the clouds. When it flew over us it made a noise like a damaged washing machine. Then it turned its nose up and climbed, and soon it was flying over the center of Concepción. There, high above the city, the plane began to write a poem in the sky. Letters of grey smoke against the rose-tinged blue of the sky, chilling the eyes of those who saw them. YOUTH . . . YOUTH, I read. I had the impression—the mad certitude—that they were printer's proofs. Then the plane swung around and flew towards us, before turning again to make another pass. This time the line was much longer and must have required great expertise on the pilot's part: IGITUR PERFECTI SUNT COELI ET TERRA ET OMNIS ORNATUS EORUM. For a moment it seemed the plane would disappear over the horizon, heading for the mountains. But it came back. One of the prisoners, a man called Norberto, who was going mad, tried to climb the wall that separated the men's yard from the women's, and started shouting: It's a Messerschmidt, a Messerschmidt fighter from the Luftwaffe. All the other prisoners stood up. The pair of guards at the door of the gymnasium, where we slept on the floor, had stopped talking and were looking at the sky. Mad Norberto, clinging to the wall, laughed and said that the Second World War had returned to the earth. It has fallen to us, the people of Chile, to greet and welcome it, he said. The plane came back over Concepción: GOOD LUCK TO EVERYONE IN DEATH, I managed to make out. For a moment I thought that if Norberto had tried to jump the wall, no one would have stopped him. Everyone else was frozen, staring up at the sky. Never in my life had I seen so much sadness. The plane came back and flew over us again; it veered around, climbed and returned to Concepción. What a pilot, said Norberto, Hans Marseille himself reincarnate. I read: DIXITQUE ADAM HOC NUNC OS EX OSSIBUS MEIS ET CARO DE CARNE MEA HAEC VOCABITUR VIRAGO QUONIAM DE VIRO SUMPTA

EST. The last letters trailed off to the east, among the clouds proceeding up the Bío-Bío valley. The plane itself disappeared completely from the sky for a moment. As if the whole thing were simply a mirage or a nightmare. I heard a miner from Lota say, What's he written, brother? No idea, came the reply. Someone else said, Just some crap; but his voice quavered. There were more policemen at the entrance to the gymnasium now: four of them. In front of me, Norberto was gripping the wall and whispering: Either this is the blitzkrieg, or I'm mad. Then he took a deep breath and seemed to calm down. The plane appeared again. We hadn't seen it turn around. Heaven forgive us our sins, said Norberto. He said it out loud, and the other prisoners and the guards heard him and laughed. But I knew that no one really felt like laughing. The plane flew over our heads. The sky was darkening; the clouds were no longer pink, but black. Over Concepción, the silhouette of the plane was barely visible. This time it wrote only three words: LEARN FROM FIRE, which quickly faded into the darkness and disappeared. For a few seconds no one said anything. The policemen were the first to react. They ordered us to get in line and began the nightly head-count before shutting us in the gymnasium. It was a Messerschmidt, Bolaño, I swear to God, Norberto said to me as we went in. Sure, I said. And it wrote in Latin, Norberto said. Yes, I said, but I didn't understand anything. I did, said Norberto, it was about Adam and Eve, and the Holy Virago, and the Garden of our heads, and he wished us all good luck. A poet, I said. Polite, anyway, said Norberto.

That joke or poem, as I was to discover many years later, cost Ramírez Hoffman a week in the guardhouse. When he got out, he kidnapped the Venegas sisters. During the festivities at the end of 1973, he put on another display of skywriting. Over the El Condor air force base, he drew a star that seemed to be one more among the early stars of dusk, and then he wrote a poem that none of his superior officers could understand. One line was about the Venegas sisters. To an informed, attentive reader, it would have been clear that the girls were already dead.

In another line he mentioned a Patricia. *Pupils of fire*, he wrote. The generals watching him release smoke to form those letters assumed that he was writing the names of his sweethearts, his friends or whores from Talcahuano. Some of his friends, however, knew that Ramírez Hoffman was conjuring up the shades of dead women. Around the same time, he participated in two further air shows. He was said to have been the most intelligent cadet in his class, and the most headstrong. He could fly a Hawker Hunter or a combat helicopter without the slightest difficulty, but what he enjoyed most was to load the old plane with smoke canisters, climb into the Fatherland's empty skies, and write out his nightmares, which were our nightmares too, for the wind to obliterate.

In 1974, having obtained the support of a general, he flew to the South Pole. It was a long and difficult voyage, but at each of his numerous refueling stops he wrote poems in the sky. According to his admirers, those poems heralded a new age of iron for the Chilean race. The Emilio Stevens who had been so reserved and unsure of himself in literary matters had disappeared without a trace. Ramírez Hoffman was confidence and audacity personified. The flight from Punta Arenas to the Arturo Prat Antarctic base was beset with dangers, which almost cost him his life. On his return, when the journalists asked him which had been the greatest danger, he replied: The stretches of silence. The waves of Cape Horn licking at the belly of the plane; huge but soundless waves, like in a silent film. Silence is like the sirens singing to Ulysses, he said, but if you resist it like a man, nothing bad can happen to you. In Antarctica everything went well. Ramírez Hoffman wrote ANTARCTICA IS CHILE, his exploit was recorded on film and in photographs, and then he returned to Concepción, on his own, in his little plane, which according to mad Norberto was a Messerschmidt from the Second World War.

He was at the height of his fame. He was called upon to undertake something grand in the capital, something spectacular to show that the new regime was interested in avant-garde art. Ramírez Hoffman was only too pleased to oblige. He stayed in the apartment of a friend from the air force academy, and spent his days training at the Captain Lindstrom airstrip, devoting his evenings to the solitary preparation of a photographic exhibition, to be held in the apartment and opened on the same day as his display of aerial poetry. Years later, the owner of the apartment declared that he had not seen the photographs Ramírez Hoffman was planning to exhibit until the night of the opening. As to the nature of the photos, he said that Ramírez Hoffman wanted to surprise the guests, and would only say that it was visual poetry—experimental, quintessential, art for art's sake—and that everyone would find it amusing. Naturally the invitations were limited: pilots, young army officers (the oldest hadn't reached the rank of commander) endowed with a certain aesthetic sensibility, a trio of journalists, a small group of civilian artists, a young society belle named Tatiana von Beck Iraola (apparently the only woman to attend the exhibition), and Ramírez Hoffman's father, who lived in Santiago.

Things got off to a bad start. On the morning of the air show, bulging black cumulus clouds rolled down the valley, heading south. Some of Ramírez Hoffman's superior officers advised him not to fly. He ignored the bad omens. He took off and the spectators watched with more apprehension than admiration as he executed a few preliminary stunts. Then he climbed and disappeared into the belly of an immense grey cloud that was moving slowly over the city. He emerged far from the airstrip, over an outlying suburb of Santiago. That was where he wrote the first line: *Death is friendship*. The he flew over some railway sheds and what appeared to be disused factories, and wrote the second line: *Death is Chile*. Then he headed for the city center. There, over the presidential palace of La Moneda, he wrote the third line: *Death is responsibility*. Some pedestrians saw him. A beetle-like silhouette against the dark and threatening sky. Very few could decipher his words: the wind effaced them almost straight away. On the way back to the airstrip he wrote the fourth and fifth lines: *Death is love* and *Death is growth*. When the strip came into sight he wrote: *Death is communion*. But none of the generals or their wives, or the senior officers, or the military, civil or cultural authorities present could read his words. A thunderstorm was brewing in the sky. From the control tower a colonel told him to hurry up and land. Ramírez Hoffman replied "Received" and immediately began to climb. Then came the lightning—the first bolt fell on the far side of Santiago—and Ramírez Hoffman wrote: *Death is cleansing*, but so unsteadily, given the adverse weather conditions, that very few of the spectators, who by now had started to get up from their seats and open their umbrellas, could understand what had been written. All that was left in the sky were dark shreds, a child's scribble. The few who did manage to make it out thought Ramírez Hoffman had gone mad. It started to rain and the crowd hurriedly dispersed. The cocktail party had to be shifted to a hangar, and by that stage, what with the delay and the downpour, everyone was in need of refreshment. In less than twenty minutes all the canapés had been devoured. Some of the officers and ladies discussed the aviator-poet's eccentric performance, but most of the conversations had moved on to questions of national and even international significance. Meanwhile Ramírez Hoffman was still up in the sky, struggling with the elements. On the airstrip glistening with rain (the scene was worthy of a Second World War film), only a handful of friends remained, and two journalists who wrote surrealist poems in their spare time, their eyes fixed on the prop plane veering around under the storm-clouds. Ramírez Hoffman wrote, or thought he wrote: *Death is my heart*. And then: *Take my heart*. And then: *Our change, our advantage*. And then he had no smoke left to write with, but still he wrote: *Death is resurrection* and the spectators were bewildered, but they knew that he was writing something. They understood the pilot's will and knew that although they couldn't make head or tail of it, they were witnessing an event of great significance for the art of the future.

Then Ramírez Hoffman landed without the slightest difficulty, was reprimanded by the officer from the control tower and certain other high-ranking officers who were still wandering among the remnants of the cocktail party, after which he went back to the apartment to prepare the second act of his Santiago gala.

The foregoing account of the air show may be reliable. Or not. Perhaps the generals of the Chilean Air Force were not accompanied by their wives. Perhaps the Captain Lindstrom airstrip was never set up for a display of aerial poetry. Perhaps Ramírez Hoffman wrote his poem in the sky over Santiago without asking permission or notifying anyone, although that seems unlikely. Perhaps it didn't even rain that day in Santiago. Perhaps it all happened differently. The following account of the photo exhibition in the apartment is, however, accurate.

The first guests arrived at nine in the evening. At 11:00, twenty people were present, all of them moderately drunk. No one had yet entered the spare bedroom, occupied by Ramírez Hoffman, on the walls of which were displayed the photos he was planning to submit to the judgment of his friends. Lieutenant Curzio Zabaleta, who years later was to publish the self-denunciatory book *Neck in a Noose*, relating his activities during the early years of the military régime, informs us that Ramírez Hoffman behaved normally, attending to the guests as if he were in his own home, greeting friends from the air force academy whom he hadn't seen for a long time, good-naturedly commenting on the morning's incidents, cheerfully cracking and tolerating the jokes that are invariably prompted by such gatherings. Now and then he disappeared (shutting himself in the spare bedroom) but he was never gone for long. Finally, on the stroke of midnight, he called for silence and said (these are his actual words, according to Zabaleta) that it was time to plunge into the art of the future. He opened the bedroom door and began to let the guests in one by one. One at a time, gentlemen; the art of Chile is not for the herd. According to Zabaleta, he said this in a jocular tone, looking at his father and winking first with his left eye, then with his right. The first person to enter the room, logically enough, was Tatiana von Beck Iraola. The room was well and normally lit. No blue or red lights, no special atmosphere. Outside, in the corridor, and back in the living room, the guests all went on talking or drinking immoderately, like the young men and the victors that they were. The smoke was thick, especially in the corridor. Ramírez Hoffman stood by the doorway. Two lieutenants were arguing in front of the bathroom. Ramírez Hoffman's father was one of the few who patiently kept his place in the line. Zabaleta, as he admitted in his confession, kept pacing nervously back and forth, filled with foreboding. The two surrealist reporters were talking with the owner of the apartment. At some point Zabaleta caught a snatch of their conversation: travel, the Mediterranean, Miami, tropical beaches, and voluptuous women.

Less than a minute after going in, Tatiana von Beck emerged from the room. She was pale and shaken. She stared at Ramírez Hoffman, then tried to get to the bathroom, unsuccessfully. After vomiting in the passage, Miss von Beck staggered to the front door with the help of an officer who gallantly offered to take her home, although she kept saying she would prefer to go alone. The second person to enter the room was a captain. He remained inside. Standing by the door, which was left ajar, Ramírez Hoffman smiled with an air of growing satisfaction. In the living room, some of the guests asked what on earth had got into Tatiana. She's just drunk, said a voice that Zabaleta didn't recognize. Someone put on a Pink Floyd record. How can you dance when there are no women? It's like a fags' convention here, someone said. The surrealist reporters whispered to each other. A lieutenant proposed they all go and find some whores straight away. Meanwhile there was hardly any talking in the hall-way, as if it were a dentist's or a nightmare's waiting room. Ramírez Hoffman's father made his way forward and went in. The owner of the apartment followed him. Almost immediately he came out again, went up to Ramírez Hoffman, and for a moment it looked as if he would hit him, but then he turned away and stormed off to the living room in search of a drink. Now everyone, including Zabaleta, pressed into the bedroom. The captain was sitting on the bed, smoking and reading some notes; he seemed calm and absorbed. Ramírez Hoffman's father was contemplating some of the hundreds of photos with which the walls and part of the ceiling had been decorated. A cadet who happened to be present, though what he was doing there Zabaleta could not explain, started crying and swearing, and had to be dragged out of the room. The surrealist reporters looked disapproving but maintained their composure. All the talking had suddenly ceased. Zabaleta remembers that the only sound was the voice of a drunken lieutenant, who hadn't yet joined the others, making a phone call in the living room. He was arguing with his girlfriend and incoherently apologizing for something he had done a long time ago. The rest of the guests went back to the living room in silence and some left hurriedly, barely taking the time to say goodbye.

Then the captain made everyone leave the room and shut himself in with Ramírez Hoffman for half an hour. According to Zabaleta, eight people were left in the apartment. Ramírez Hoffman's father didn't seem particularly disturbed. Slumped in an armchair, the owner of the apartment looked at him resentfully. If you like, said Ramírez Hoffman's father, I'll take my son away. No, said the owner of the apartment, your son is my friend, and friendship is sacred in Chile. He was completely drunk.

A couple of hours later three military intelligence agents arrived. Zabaleta thought they would arrest Ramírez Hoffman, but what they did was go into the bedroom and clear away the photographs. The captain left with the agents, and for a while no one knew what to say. Then Ramírez Hoffman emerged from the bedroom, walked over to the window and lit a cigarette. The room, Zabaleta recalls, felt like the looted cold-storage vault of a giant butcher's shop. Are you under arrest? the owner of the apartment finally asked. I guess so, said Ramírez Hoffman, without turning to face them, looking out at the lights of Santiago, the sparsely scattered lights of Santiago. With painfully slow movements, as if he had to gather his courage, Ramírez Hoffman's father drew near and finally gave him a quick hug. Ramírez Hoffman did not respond. Why the drama? asked one of the surrealist reporters beside the ashen hearth. You can shut up, said the owner of the apartment. What do we do now? asked a lieutenant. Sleep it off, replied the host. Zabaleta never saw Ramírez Hoffman again. But that last image was indelible: the big living room a mess; bottles, plates and overflowing ashtrays, a group of pale, exhausted men, and Ramírez Hoffman at the window, showing no sign of fatigue, with a glass of whisky in his perfectly steady hand, contemplating the dark cityscape.

The reports of Ramírez Hoffman's activities from that night on are vague and contradictory. His shadowy figure makes a number of brief appearances in the shifting anthology of Chilean literature, always enveloped in mist, elegant as a dragon. According to some rumors, he was expelled from the air force. The most unbalanced minds of his generation claimed to have seen him wandering around Santiago, Valparaíso, and Concepción, working at a variety of jobs and participating in strange artistic projects. He changed his name. He was associated with various ephemeral literary magazines, to which he contributed proposals for happenings that never happened, unless (and it hardly bears thinking about) he organized them in secret. A theatrical magazine published a short play by a certain Octavio Pacheco, who was a mystery to everyone. This play is odd, to say the very least, and the action unfolds in a world inhabited exclusively by Siamese twins, where sadism and masochism are children's games. Ramírez Hoffman was said to be working as a pilot for a commercial airline whose flights linked South America with certain cities in the Far East. Cecilio Macaduck, poet and shoe-store salesman, followed his trail thanks to a document-storage box he happened to discover at the National Library, containing the only two poems published by Emilio Stevens, photographic records of Ramírez Hoffman's aerial poems, Octavio Pacheco's works for the theatre, and texts that had appeared in various magazines in Argentina, Uruguay, Brazil and Chile. Macaduck was flabbergasted: he found at least seven Chilean magazines published between 1973 and 1980 that he'd never heard of. He also came across a slender octavo volume entitled *Interview with Juan Sauer*. The book bore the imprint of The Fourth Reich in Argentina. It didn't take long to ascertain that Juan Sauer, who spoke in the interview about photography and poetry, was none other than Ramírez Hoffman. In his replies he sketched out a theory of art. Disappointing, according to Macaduck. Yet in certain literary circles, both in Chile and elsewhere in Latin America, his poetic career, brief and dazzling as a lightning bolt, inspired a kind of cult, in spite of the fact that few devotees had an accurate idea of what he had written. Finally he left Chile behind, along with public life, and disappeared, although his physical absence (he had, in fact, *always* been an absent figure) did not put a stop to the speculations and interpretations, the passionate and contradictory readings to which his work gave rise.

His passage through literature left a trail of blood and several questions posed by a mute. It also left one or two silent replies.

Rather than sinking into oblivion with the passing years, he became a mythic figure and his ideas found a wider following. His traces petered out in South Africa, Germany, Italy; some even went so far as to claim that he had gone to Japan, as if to be Gary Snyder's dark double. His silence was absolute. Yet the winds of change blowing through the world were favorable to him and his work, and some came to see him as a precursor. Young, enthusiastic writers set out from Chile in search of him. They returned from their long pilgrimages broke and empty-handed. Ramírez Hoffman's father, presumably the one person who knew his whereabouts, died in 1990.

As the years went by, it was gradually supposed in Chilean literary circles that Ramírez Hoffman was dead too, a reassuring thought for many.

In 1992, his name appeared prominently in a judicial report on torture and the disappearance of prisoners. In 1993 he was linked to an "independent operational group" responsible for the deaths of various students in and around Concepción and Santiago. In 1995, Zabaleta published his book, one chapter of which described the photographic exhibition. In 1996, a small press in Santiago published Cecilio Macaduck's lengthy study of Fascist magazines in Chile and Argentina between 1972 and 1992, in which the brightest and most enigmatic star, without a doubt, is Ramírez Hoffman. Naturally there were people who spoke out in his defense. A sergeant from Military Intelligence declared that Lieutenant Ramírez Hoffman was a little strange, slightly unhinged and prone to unexpected outbursts, but exemplary in his commitment to the fight against Communism. An army officer who had taken part in a number of counter-subversive operations with Ramírez Hoffman in Santiago went further still and affirmed that he had been absolutely right to say that no prisoner who had been tortured should be left alive: "His vision of History, you understand, was, how can I put it, cosmic, in perpetual motion, with Nature in the midst of it all, devouring itself and being reborn, repugnant but nothing short of brilliant. . . ."

Ramírez Hoffman was called as a witness in a number of trials, although no one expected him to show up. In other cases he was indicted. A judge in Concepción tried to obtain a warrant for his arrest, unsuccessfully. The few trials that went ahead were conducted in his absence. And soon they were forgotten. The Republic had too many problems to concern itself for long with the fading figure of a serial killer who had disappeared years ago.

Chile forgot him.

This is where Abel Romero appears on the scene and I make my reappearance. Chile had forgotten us as well. During the time of Allende, Romero had been something of a celebrity in the police force. I vaguely remembered his name in connection with a murder in Viña del Mar, a "classic locked-room murder," as he put it himself, neatly and elegantly solved. And although he always worked in homicide, he was the one who went into the Las Carmenes estate to "rescue" a colonel who had staged his own kidnapping, and was being protected by several thugs from the right-wing group Patria y Libertad. This operation earned Romero the Medal of Valor, awarded by Allende in person: the high point of his professional life. After the coup, he was imprisoned for three years, and when he got out he went to Paris. Now he was on Ramírez Hoffman's trail. Cecilio Macaduck had given him my address in Barcelona. How can I help you, I asked him. By advising me on poetic matters, he said. This was his reasoning: Ramírez Hoffman was a poet, I was a poet, he was not. To find a poet, he needed the help of another poet. I told him that in my opinion Ramírez Hoffman was a criminal, not a poet. All right, all right, maybe in Ramírez Hoffman's opinion, or anyone else's for that matter, *you're* not a poet, or a bad one, and he's the real thing. It all depends, don't you think? How much are you going to pay me? I asked. That's the way, he said, straight to the point. Quite a bit: my client isn't short of money. We became friends. The next day he came to my apartment with a suitcase full of literary magazines. What makes you think he's in Europe? I know his profile, he said. Four days later he turned up with a television and a VCR. These are for you, he said. I don't watch television, I said. Well you should, you don't know what you're missing. I read books and I write, I said. And it shows, said Romero. I don't mean that as an insult, he added immediately, I've always respected priests and writers who own nothing. You can't have known many, I said. You're the first. Then he explained that he couldn't really set up the television in the boarding house where he was staying, in the Calle Pintor Fortuny. Do you think Ramírez Hoffman writes in French or German, I asked. Maybe, he said, he was an educated man.

Among the many magazines that Romero left me were two in which I thought I could see the hand of Ramírez Hoffman. One was French and the other was published in Madrid by a group of Argentineans. The French one, no more than a fanzine, was the official organ of a movement known as "barbaric writing" whose major exponent was a retired Parisian concierge. One of the movement's activities was to hold black masses in which classic books were mistreated. The ex-concierge began his career in May 1968. While the students were building barricades, he shut himself in his cubicle-like caretaker's apartment and devoted himself to masturbating onto books by Victor Hugo and Balzac, urinating onto Stendhal novels, smearing shit over pages of Chateaubriand, cutting various parts of his body and spattering the blood over handsome editions of Flaubert, Lamartine or Musset. That, so he claimed, was how he learned to write. The group of "barbaric writers" was made up of sales assistants, butchers, security guards, locksmiths, lowly bureaucrats, nursing aides and movie extras. The Madrid magazine, by contrast, was of a higher standard and its contributors could not be lumped together under a specific tendency or school. In its pages I found texts on psychoanalysis, studies of the New Christianity, and poems written by prisoners in the Carabanchel jail, preceded by an ingenious and at times extravagant sociological introduction. One of those poems, clearly the best, and the longest, was entitled "The Photographer of Death" and was dedicated, mysteriously, *To the explorer.*

In the French magazine the works of the "barbarians" were accompanied by a few enthusiastic critical texts, in one of which I thought I could see the shadow of Ramírez Hoffman. It was signed by a certain Jules Defoe and argued, in a jerky and ferocious style, that literature should be written by non-literary people (just as politics should be and indeed was being taken over by non-politicians, as the author was delighted to observe). The impending revolution in writing would, in a sense, abolish literature itself. When poetry is written by non-poets and read by non-readers. Anyone could have written that text, I knew, anyone determined to set the world alight; but something told me that this particular apostle of the Parisian ex-concierge was Ramírez Hoffman.

The poem by the prisoner from Carabanchel cast a different light on the matter. In the Madrid magazine there were no texts by Ramírez Hoffman, but there was one about him, although it did not mention his name. I thought the title, "The Photographer of Death," might have been borrowed from an old film by Powell or Pressburger, I couldn't remember which, but it might also have been an allusion to Ramírez Hoffman's onetime hobby. Essentially, in spite of the subjectivity clogging its lines, the poem was simple: it was about a photographer roaming the world, the crimes retained forever in the photographer's mechanical eye, the planet's sudden emptiness, the photographer's boredom, his ideals (the absolute) and wanderings through unknown lands, his experiences with women, and interminable evenings and nights given over to the observation of love in all its varied configurations: pairs, threesomes, groups.

After I told Romero about this, he asked me to watch four movies on the VCR he had brought. I think we have located Mr. Ramírez, he said. At that moment I felt scared. We started watching the movies together. They were low-budget porn. Halfway through the second one, I told Romero I couldn't take four porn movies in a row. Watch them tonight, he said on his way out. Am I supposed to recognize Ramírez Hoffman? Is he one of the actors? He smiled enigmatically and left, after noting down the addresses of the magazines I had singled out for him. I didn't see him again until five days later. In the meantime I watched all the movies, and I watched them all more than once. Ramírez Hoffman didn't appear in any of them. But I could feel his presence in them all. It's very simple, Romero said when we met again, the lieutenant is behind the camera. Then he told me the story of a crew that used to make pornographic films in a villa on the Gulf of Tarento. One morning they were all found dead. Six people in all. Three actresses, two actors and the cameraman. The prime suspect was the director-producer, who was taken into custody. They also arrested the owner of the villa, a lawyer from Corigliano who was associated with the underworld of violent hard-core: porn showing real criminal acts. Both had alibis and had to be released. And what did Ramírez Hoffman have to do with all this? There was a second cameraman. A certain R. P. English. And he had never been tracked down.

Would you be able to recognize Ramírez Hoffman if you saw him again? asked Romero. I don't know, I replied.

Two months went by before I saw Romero again. I've tracked down Jules Defoe, he said: Let's go. I followed him without saying a word. I hadn't ventured out of Barcelona for a long time. To my surprise, we took the train that runs along the coast. Who's paying you? I asked him. A Chilean, said Romero, looking out at the Mediterranean appearing in flashes between empty factories and then behind the first building sites of the Maresme. A lot? A fair bit; he's made a fortune, he sighed. Apparently quite a few people are getting rich in Chile these days. And what are you going to do with the money? I'm going back; it'll help me to start over. Your client wouldn't be Cecilio Macaduck by any chance? (For a moment I thought that Cecilio Macaduck, who had stayed in Chile, and now published a book every two years, contributed to magazines all over the continent and occasionally gave guest lectures at small North American universities—for a moment, as I say, I thought that Macaduck, as well as becoming an established writer, had become wealthy. It was a moment of idiocy and justifiable envy.) No way, said Romero. And when we find him, what are you going to do? I asked. Ah, Bolaño my friend, first you have to recognize him.

We got off the train in Blanes. At the station we took a bus to Lloret. Spring had only just begun but already there were groups of tourists gathered around the doors of the hotels and sauntering along the main streets of the village. We walked towards a neighborhood full of apartment buildings. In one of them lived Ramírez Hoffman. Are you going to kill him? I asked as we walked down a spectral street. The tourist shops wouldn't open for another month yet. Don't ask me questions like that, said Romero, his face creased with pain or something similar. All right, I said, no more questions.

This is where Ramírez Hoffman lives, said Romero, as we walked past an apparently empty, eight-story building, without stopping. My stomach clenched. Hey, don't look back, he scolded, and we kept walking. Two blocks further on there was a bar open. Romero came to the door with me. He'll come here for a coffee in a while, I can't say when exactly. Have a good look at him and then you can tell me. Yes,

I said. See you soon, and remember, it's more than twenty years ago.

From the front windows of the bar, there was a view of the sea, with a few fishing boats at work near the coast, under an intensely blue sky. I ordered a coffee with milk and tried to concentrate. The bar was almost empty: there was a woman sitting at a table reading a magazine and two men talking with the bartender. I opened my book, *The Complete Works of Bruno Schulz,* translated by Juan Carlos Vidal. I tried to read. After a few pages I realized I wasn't understanding anything. I was reading, but the words went scuttling past like incomprehensible beetles. Nobody came into the bar; nobody moved. Time seemed to be standing still. I started to feel sick; the fishing boats on the sea had turned into yachts; the beach was uniformly grey and every once in a while someone walked or cycled past on the broad, empty pavement. I ordered a bottle of mineral water. Then Ramírez Hoffman came in and sat down by the front window, three tables away. He had aged. Like me, I suppose. But no, much more than me. He was fatter, more wrinkled; he looked at least ten years older than I did, although in fact there was a difference of only three years between us. He was staring at the sea and smoking. Just like me, I realized with a fright, stubbing out my cigarette and pretending to read. But Bruno Schulz's words had taken on a monstrous character that was almost intolerable. When I looked again at Ramírez Hoffman, he had turned sideways. It struck me that he had a hard look peculiar to certain Latin Americans over the age of forty. A sad, irreparable sort of hardness. But Ramírez Hoffman did not appear to be sad, and that is precisely where the infinite sadness lay. He seemed *adult.* But he wasn't adult, I knew that straight away. He seemed self-possessed. And in his own way, on his own terms, whatever they were, he was more self-possessed than the rest of us in that sleepy bar, or most of the people walking through the streets of Lloret or working to get ready for the imminent tourist season. He was hard, he had nothing or very little, and it didn't seem to bother him much. He seemed to be going through a rough patch. He had the face of a man who knows how to wait without losing his nerve or letting his imagination run wild. He didn't look like a poet. He didn't look like he had been an officer in the Chilean Air Force. He didn't look like an infamous killer. He didn't look like a man who had flown to Antarctica to write a poem in the sky. Not at all.

As it was starting to get dark, he left. Suddenly I felt light-hearted and hungry. I ordered bread with tomato and ham, and a non-alcoholic beer.

Romero arrived shortly and we left together. At first we seemed to be going away from Ramírez Hoffman's building, but in fact we just circled around to it. Is it him? asked Romero. Yes, I said. Are you certain? I'm certain. I was going to say something more, but Romero quickened his pace. Ramírez Hoffman's building loomed against the sky, lit by the moon. It was somehow different from the buildings around it, which seemed to be losing definition, fading, as if under a magic spell dating back to 1973. Romero pointed to a park bench. Wait for me here, he said. Are you going to kill him? The bench was tucked away in a shadowy corner. I couldn't see the expression on Romero's face. Wait for me here or go to the station in Blanes and take the first train. Please don't kill him, he's not going to do any more harm now, I said. You don't know that, said Romero, nor do I. He can't hurt anyone now, I said. But I didn't really believe it. Of course he could. We all could. I'll be right back, said Romero.

As the sound of his footfalls grew fainter, I sat there looking at the dark shrubs. Twenty minutes later he returned with a folder under his arm. Let's go, he said. We took the bus from Lloret back to Blanes and then the train to Barcelona. We didn't talk until we reached the Plaza Cataluña station. Romero came back to my apartment. There he gave me an envelope. For your trouble, he said. What are you going to do? I'm going back to Paris tonight, he said, I've got a flight at midnight. I sighed or snorted. What an ugly business, I said, for something to say. Naturally, said Romero, it was Chilean business. I looked at him standing there in the entranceway; he was smiling. He must have been going on sixty. Look after yourself, Bolaño, he said, and off he went.

# EPILOGUE FOR MONSTERS

## 1. Secondary Figures

Marcos Ricardo Alarcón Chamiso. Arequipa, 1910–Arequipa, 1977. Poet, musician, painter, sculptor and amateur mathematician.

Susy D'Amato. Buenos Aires, 1935–Paris, 2001. Argentinean poet and friend of Luz Mendiluce. She ended her days selling Latin American handcrafts in the French capital.

Duchess of Bahamontes. Cordoba, 1893–Madrid, 1957. Duchess and Cordoban. Period. Her (platonic) lovers numbered in the hundreds. Urinary problems and anorgasmia. A fine gardener in her old age.

Pedro Barbero. Móstoles, 1934–Madrid, 1998. Secretary, lover and confidant of Luz Mendiluce. The Miguel Hernández of the populist right. Author of proletarian sonnets.

Gabino Barreda. Hermosillo, 1908–Los Angeles, 1989. Renowned architect. He began as a Stalinist and ended as a Salinist, supporting Carlos Salinas de Gortari.

Tatiana von Beck Iraola. Santiago, 1950–Santiago, 2011. Feminist, gallery owner, journalist, conceptual sculptor, one of the pillars of Chilean cultural life.

Luis Enrique Belmar. Buenos Aires, 1865–Buenos Aires, 1940. Literary critic. He declared that Macedonio Fernández couldn't write to save his life. Savage in his treatment of Edelmira Thompson.

Hugo Bossi. Buenos Aires, 1920–Buenos Aires, 1991. Architect. Creator of the Museum-Hotel projects, which were, he confessed, inspired by his years as a boarder at a Jesuit school in the Province of Buenos Aires. The Museum-Hotel, as well as being a museum open to the public and a residence for artists in need, was to have various subterranean sports grounds, a velodrome, a cinema, two theaters, a chapel, a supermarket, and a small, discreet police station.

Jack Brooke. New Jersey, 1950–Los Angeles, 1990. Art dealer associated with the drug trade and money-laundering. Declaimer and quick-change artist in his spare time.

Mauricio Cáceres. Tres Arroyos, 1925–Buenos Aires, 1996. Second husband of Luz Mendiluce. Popularly known as The Martín Fierro of the Apocalypse. Onetime editor of *American Letters*.

Florencio Capó. Concepción, 1920–Santiago, 1995. Friend and confidant of Pedro González Carrera. Although very fond of González, he could never understand his friend's posthumous fame.

Dan Carmine. Los Angeles, 1958–Los Angeles, 1986. Extremely well-endowed porn actor. His penis was eleven and a half inches long. He had the bluest eyes in the business, and worked in several of Adolfo Pantoliano's films.

Aldo Carozzone. Buenos Aires, 1893–Buenos Aires, 1982. Epicurean philosopher and private secretary to Edelmira Thompson.

Edelmiro Carozzone. Buenos Aires, 1940–Madrid, 2027.The only child of Aldo Carozzone. He was originally to be named Adolfo (after Adolph Hilter), but at the last minute, his father chose instead the name of his employer and benefactor, as a mark of his devoted friendship. As a boy he was perpetually amazed and fitfully happy. He later worked as a secretary to the Mendiluce family.

John Castellano. Mobile 1950–Selma, 2021. North American writer. Dubbed *The Duce of Alabama* by Argentino Schiaffino.

Enzo Raúl Castiglioni. Buenos Aires, 1940–Buenos Aires, 2002. Leader of the Boca Juniors soccer gang. When he was imprisoned, his place was taken by Italo Schiaffino. Closely resembled a rat, according to some of his contemporaries. A hybrid of rat and peacock, according to others. A pathetic loser, in the opinion of his family.

Juan Cherniakovski. Valdivia, 1943–El Salvador, 1984. Panamerican poet and guerrila fighter. Second cousin of the Soviet general Ivan Cherniakovski.

Arthur Crane. New Orleans, 1947–Los Angeles, 1989. Poet. Author of a number of important books, including *Homosexual Heaven* and *Disciplining Children*. He indulged his suicidal tendencies by frequenting the underworld and hanging out with lowlifes. Others smoke three packs of cigarettes a day.


Eugenio Entrescu. Bacau, Rumania, 1905–Kishinev, Ukraine, 1944. Rumanian General. During the Second World War he distinguished himself in the capture of Odessa, the Siege of Sebastopol and the Battle of Stalingrad. Erect, his member was exactly twelve inches long, half an inch longer than that of Dan Carmine. He commanded the 20th Division, the 14th Division and the 3rd Infantry Corps. His soldiers crucified him in a village near Kishinev.

Atilio Franchetti. Buenos Aires, 1919–Buenos Aires, 1990. Painter who took part in the *Poe's Room* project.

Persio de la Fuente. Buenos Aires, 1919–Buenos Aires, 1990. Argentinean colonel and eminent semiologist.


Honesto García. Buenos Aires, 1950–Buenos Aires, 2013. Onetime hit man and leader of the Boca soccer gang. Died a beggar, bawling tangos, crying and shitting in his pants in an out-of-the-way street in Villa Devoto.

Martín García. Los Angeles, Chile, 1942–Perpignan, 1989. Chilean poet and translator. His writing workshop held in the Concepción medical faculty was one of the world's most disgusting phenomena: two steps away, across the corridor, was the operating theater where the anatomy students were dissecting corpses.

María Teresa Greco. New Jersey, 1936–Orlando, 2004. Argentino Schiaffino's second wife. According to eye-witnesses she was tall, thin and bony, a sort of ghost or incarnation of the will.

Wenceslao Hassel. Pando, Uruguay, 1900–Montevideo, 1958. Playwright. Author of *America's Domestic Wars, How to Be a Man, Ferocity, Argentinean Women in Paris* and other plays, applauded in their day by theater audiences in Buenos Aires, Montevideo and Santiago de Chile.

Otto Haushofer. Berlin, 1871–Berlin, 1945. Nazi philosopher. Godfather of Luz Mendiluce and father of various harebrained theories: hollow earth, solid universe, original civilizations, the interplanetary Aryan tribe. He committed suicide after being raped by three drunk Uzbek soldiers.


Antonio Lacouture. Buenos Aires, 1943–Buenos Aires, 1999. Argentinean military officer. He defeated subversives but lost the Falklands. An expert in the "submarine" technique and the application of electrodes. He invented a game using mice. The sound of his voice made prisoners tremble. He received various decorations.

Julio César Lacouture. Buenos Aires, 1927–Buenos Aires, 1984. Luz Mendiluce's first husband. Author of an "Ode to San Martín" and an "Ode to O'Higgins," which both won municipal prizes.


Juan José Lasa Mardones. Cuban poet whose life is a mystery, with scattered poems to his name. Possibly invented by Ernesto Pérez Masón.

Philippe Lemercier. Nevers, 1925–Buenos Aires, 1984. French landscape painter and editor of Ignacio Zubieta's posthumous works.

Juan Carlos Lentini. Buenos Aires, 1945–Buenos Aires, 2008. Onetime soccer gang leader. He finished his days as a federal government employee.

Carola Leyva. Mar del Plata, 1945–Mar del Plata, 2018. Argentinean poet and follower of Edelmira Thompson and Luz Mendiluce.

Susana Lezcano Lafinur. Buenos Aires, 1867–Buenos Aires, 1949. Hostess. Her salon was one of the institutions of cultural life in Buenos Aires.

Marcus Long. Pittsburgh, 1928–Phoenix, 1989. Poet whose work successively resembled that of Charles Olson, Robert Lowell, W. S. Merwin, Kenneth Rexroth and Lawrence Ferlinghetti. Literature professor. Father of Rory Long.

Cecilio Macaduck. Concepción, 1956–Santiago, 2021. Chilean writer whose curious work, characterized by abundant detail and ominous atmospheres, has won him an enthusiastic following among critics and general readers. Until the age of thirty-three he worked as a sales assistant in a shoe store.

Berta Macchio Morazán. Buenos Aires, 1960–Mar del Plata, 2029. Amateur illustrator. Niece and lover of Dr. Morazán. Also the lover of Argentino Schiaffino. Highly strung. Her relationships with the aforementioned individuals resulted in committal to an insane asylum and several suicide attempts. Doctor Morazán liked to tie her to the bed or to a chair. Argentino Schiaffino preferred the more traditional slaps, or stubbing out cigarettes on her arms and legs. She was also the lover of Scotti Cabello and occasionally eight or nine longtime members of the Boca soccer gang. Morazán always said that he loved her like a daughter.

Alfredo de María. Mexico City, 1962–Villaviciosa, 2022. Science fiction writer. Gustavo Borda's neighbor in Los Angeles for two interminable years. Disappeared in Villaviciosa, a village of killers in the state of Sonora.

Pedro de Medina. Guadalajara, 1920–Mexico City, 1989. Mexican novelist whose themes were the revolution and the rural poor.

Sebastián Mendiluce. Buenos Aires, 1874–Buenos Aires, 1940. Argentinean millionaire. Husband of Edelmira Thompson.

Carlos Enrique Morazán. Buenos Aires, 1940–Buenos Aires, 2004. Leader of the Boca soccer gang after the death of Italo Schiaffino and devoted admirer of Italo's younger brother Argentino. Doctor of parapsychology.

Elizabeth Moreno. Miami, 1974–Miami, 2040. Waitress in a Cuban café. Third and last wife of Argentino Schiaffino.

Adolfo Pantoliano. Vallejo, California, 1945–Los Angeles, 1986. Director and producer of pornographic movies. Works: *Hot Bunnies, Stick It In My Ass, The Ex-Cons and the Horny Fifteen-Year-Old, Three By Three*, and *Alien Versus Corina*, among others.

Agustín Pérez Heredia. Buenos Aires, 1935–Buenos Aires, 2005. Argentinean Fascist associated with the world of sport.

Jorge Esteban Petrovich. Buenos Aires, 1960–Buenos Aires, 2027. Author of three war novels set in the Falklands. Radio and television presenter in later life.

Jules Albert Ramis. Rouen, 1910–Paris, 1995. Prize-winning French poet. Held an official post in Petain's government. Revisionist. Sporadic and gifted translator from English and Spanish. Member of Parliament. Philosopher in his spare time. Patron of the arts. Founder of the Mandarins' Club.

Julián Rico Anaya. Junín, 1942–Buenos Aires, 1998. Argentinean author. Nationalist and ultra-Catholic.

Baldwin Rocha. Los Angeles, 1999–Laguna Beach, 2017. Killed Rory Long with an assault rifle. Died three minutes later under a hail of gunfire from Long's bodyguards.

Abel Romero. Puerto Montt, 1940–Santiago, 2013. Chilean ex-policeman who spent many years in exile. On his return he established a successful firm of funeral directors.

Étienne de Saint Étienne. Lyon, 1920–Paris, 1999. French philosopher and revisionist historian. Founder of *The Review of Contemporary History*.

Claudia Saldaña. Rosario, 1955–Rosario, 1976. Argentinean poet. Unpublished. Killed by the military regime.

Ximena San Diego. Buenos Aires, 1870–Paris, 1938. Fossilized gaucho version of Nina de Villard.

Lou Santino. San Bernadino, 1940–San Bernadino, 2006. John Lee Brook's parole officer. According to some, Brook among them, a saint. According to others, a cynical son of a bitch.

Germán Scotti Cabello. Buenos Aires, 1956–Buenos Aires, 2017. Dr. Morazán's right-hand man and unconditional admirer of Argentino Schiaffino.

André Thibault. Niort, 1880–Périgueux, 1945. Philosopher and follower of Maurras. Executed by a group of resistance fighters in the Périgord.

Alcides Urrutia. Cuban painter of whom nothing more is known. Likely guest in Castro's jails. Another of Ernesto Pérez Masón's inventions?

Tito Vásquez. Rosario, 1895–Río de Janeiro, 1957. Argentinean musician. Composer of symphonies, various chamber works, three hymns, a funeral march, a sonatina, and eight tangos that permitted him to live out his days in dignity.
Arturo Velasco. Buenos Aires, 1921–Paris, 1983. Argentinean painter. He began as a Symbolist and ended up imitating Le Parc.
Magdalena Venegas. Nacimiento, 1955–Concepción, 1973. Chilean poet. Twin sister of María Venegas. Killed by the military regime.
María Venegas. Nacimiento, 1955–Concepción, 1973. Chilean poet. Killed by the military regime.

Susy Webster. Berkeley, 1960–Los Angeles, 1986. Porn star. Worked in several of of Adolfo Pantoliano's films.

Curzio Zabaleta. Santiago, 1951–Viña del Mar, 2011. Retired Chilean Air Force captain. Lay monk. Author of bucolic and ecological works.
Augusto Zamora. San Luis Potosí, 1919–Mexico City, 1969. Known as a social-realist author, although he wrote surrealist poems in secret. He was homosexual, although he kept up a macho pretence almost all his life. For more than twenty years he fooled his colleagues into believing that he could speak Russian. He saw the light in 1968, in a cell in the Lecumberri prison. He died in the street of a heart attack a month after being released.

## 2. Publishing Houses, Magazines, Places . . .

*American Letters.* Bimonthly magazine founded by Edelmira Thompson, 1948-1979. It was co-edited by Juan and Luz Mendiluce, which gave rise to inter-sibling quarrels.

Black and White. Extreme right-wing Argentinean publishing house.

Black Pistol. Publishing house based in Rio de Janeiro, specializing in detective fiction, which opened the door to a large and disparate group of Brazilian writers.

The Charismatic Church of Californian Christians. Religious congregation founded by Rory Long in 1984.

The Chestnut. Argentinean publishing house specializing in songbooks and popular authors.

Church of the True Martyrs of America. Religious congregation in which Rory Long was a preacher.

City in Flames. Poetry publishing house based in Macon.

*Command.* War games magazine to which Harry Sibelius contributed.

*Dawn in California.* One of the Aryan Brotherhood's magazines.

*The Fabulous Adventures of the White Nation.* One of the Aryan brotherhood's magazines.

*The Fourth Reich in Argentina.* No doubt one of the most peculiar, outlandish and stubborn publishing ventures spawned by the Americas, ever fecund in enterprises verging on insanity, illegality and idiocy. The topical first issue was entirely devoted to refuting the legality of the Nuremberg trials, which were in full swing at the time. In the second issue, among translations of entirely forgettable German authors (including a poem about gardenias by Baldur von Schirach, leader of the Hitler Youth, then on trial in Nuremberg for crimes against humanity), the enterprising reader may discover three disparate prose texts by Ernst Jünger. A double issue followed, returning to the theme of the trials and presenting a brief anthology of conspicuously Falangist and Peronist poets from Buenos Aires. The hundred pages of the fifth issue are entirely occupied by an exposé and analysis of the Bolshevik menace, the only real threat to Europe since the end of the First World War. With the sixth issue, the style of the magazine took a new turn: the theme is old Buenos Aires and its neighborhoods, the port, the river, the city's traditions and folklore. In a fit of speculation, the seventh issue envisaged the Buenos Aires of the future, its urban planning (imagined by the young architect Hugo Bossi, with the first glimmers of an implacable originality that would later make him world famous), but also its sociology, economics and politics. The eighth issue came down to earth again, railing, from cover to cover, against the fallacies of the Nuremberg trials and the total control of the press by the Jewish plutocracy. The ninth issue returned to literature: under the title "European Literature Today," it gives a brief overview of the works of French, German, Italian, Spanish, Rumanian, Lithuanian, Slovakian, Hungarian, Belgian, Latvian and Danish writers and poets. A police warrant prevented the publication of the tenth issue. The magazine was outlawed but transformed itself into a publishing house. Some titles appeared under the imprint of the Fourth Reich in Argentina, but the majority did not. In its new guise the Fourth Reich continued to make its erratic way until the year 2001. The identity of the publisher remains a mystery.

*The General.* War games magazine to which Harry Sibelius contributed.

*History and Thought.* Chilean magazine whose early issues contained articles and essays on European and American geopolitics and military history. Under the editorship of Gunther Füchler, no doubt the magazine's most ambitious and inventive editor, *History and Thought* attempted to launch the careers of a series of German-Chilean novelists and short-story writers (Axel Axelrod, Basilio Rodríguez de la Mata, Herman Cueto Bauer, Otto Munsen, Rodolfo Ernesto Gruber, etc.) with results that were initially mixed but constituted overall and in the end a resounding flop: only two of the authors persisted in their literary endeavors beyond the age of twenty-five, one of them opting to write in German, and, unsurprisingly, in Germany. The magazine's first editor, J.C. Hoeffler, was responsible for a *Public History of the Second World War*, followed by a *Secret History of the Second World War*, not to mention the first respectable Spanish translation of Baldur von Schirach's *Selected Poems*. Werner Méndez Maier, editor from 1979 to 1980, a ferocious futurist whose ready fists drove away the editorial board and the magazine's sponsors, was the author of the controversial *Lieutenant Ramírez Hoffman: News from Reliable Sources*, which at the time was considered by friends and enemies alike as a monumental and quasi-schizophrenic exercise in leg-pulling. Gunther Füchler, the third editor (from 1980 to 1989), was the author of an enormous *History of Pacific War*, devoted to the conflict between Chile and the alliance of Peru and Bolivia in 1879, a 740-page tome aspiring to exhaustiveness, which includes minute descriptions of everything from the uniforms of both sides to the strategic, operational and tactical battle plans. In 1997 the National Literary Prize was awarded to Füchler in recognition of his historical labors, a high point in the career of the magazine's most respected general editor. Under Karl-Heinz Riddle, *History and Thought* entered a more openly revisionist phase. It was influenced by the thinking and theories of the French philosopher Étienne de Saint-Étienne, a controversial professor at the University of Lyon, who tried to use historical documents (including dubious permits for the opening of kosher butchers' shops) to prove that only 300,000 Jews had died in all the concentration camps during the Second World War. Following in Saint-Étienne's footsteps, Riddle produced a miscellaneous series of eccentric articles in which the historico-mathematical-enumerative system was taken to its ultimate consequences. The decline which had shown early signs in Riddle's time was finally confirmed under the editorship of Antonio Capistrano (1998–2003), a poet in the Georgian style, formerly associated with the *Southern Hemisphere Literary Review*, whose sole quality was administrative efficiency. At the beginning of the twenty-first century, the German-Chilean axis was no longer able to provide funds or generate enthusiasm, and the die-hards continued their crusade on the information superhighways.

*The Hotel of the Brave*. One of the Aryan Brotherhood's magazines.

*The Inner Circle*. One of the Aryan Brotherhood's magazines.

*Iron Heart*. Chilean Nazi magazine which survived for a number of years not in an Antarctic submarine base, as its ardent instigators would have preferred, but in Punta Arenas.

Lamp of the South. Publishing house founded by Edelmira Thompson. 1920–1946. Never made a cent.

*Literature behind Bars*. One of the Aryan Brotherhood's magazines.

*Living Poetry*. Literary magazine published in Cartagena, Spain, 1938–1947.

The Mandarins' Club. Metaphysical and literary group created by Jules Albert Ramis.

*Modern Argentina*. Monthly magazine founded by Edelmira Thompson and initially edited by Adlo Carozzone.

The Naturalist Aryan Commune. Founded (in 1967) by Segundo José Heredia on a farm near Calabozo (in the state of Guárico), where Frank Zwickau and other Venezuelan artists of vaguely Aryan extraction put up for a few days.

*The Poetic and Literary Beacon*. Magazine published in Seville, 1934–1944.

*Second Round*. Literary and sporting magazine founded and edited by Segundo José Heredia, which brought together a large and generally ungrateful group of young Venezuelan writers.

*Southern Hemisphere Literary Review*. When Ezequiel Arancibia and Juan Herring Lazo embarked on their publishing venture, their aim was not only to provide an alternative to *History and Thought*, but also a Chilean response to that journal's

Germanic thrust. As they saw it, *History and Thought's* team represented German National Socialism, while the following they hoped to gather would represent Fascism. An Italian, aestheticist, swaggering Fascism in the case of Arancibia; while Herring Lazo espoused a Spanish, Catholic, Falangist, anti-capitalist Fascism in the style of Primo de Rivera. Politically, they were stalwart supporters of Pinochet, although they did not spare him their "loyal criticism," especially in regard to economic matters. In literature they admired only Pedro González Carrera, whose complete works they edited. Unlike the Germanists of *History and Thought*, they did not disdain Pablo Neruda and Pablo de Rokha; indeed they made a methodical study of Neruda and de Rokha's free verse, with its long lines and powerful cadences, and often cited the pair as exemplary practitioners of militant poetry. All you had to do was change a few names—Mussolini instead of Stalin, Stalin instead of Trotsky—slightly adjust the adjectives, replace a few nouns, and you had the ideal pamphlet poem, a genre they recommended as salutary given the historical context, although they never granted it the supreme place of honor. By contrast they loathed the poetry of Nicanor Parra and Enrique Lihn, which they considered hollow and decadent, heartless and despairing. They were excellent translators and introduced the Chilean public to the work of many lesser-known poets writing in English, German, French, Italian, Portuguese, Rumanian, Flemish, Swedish and even Afrikaans (a language that Arancibia taught himself, according to his friends, with the help of a good dictionary and three trips to South Africa). In the early days they tried to promote only artists with whom they had political as well as literary affinities, and aggressively dismissed all other schools of thought. They organized readings and literary events in the provinces, venturing to remote regions devoid of literary tradition, where the low rates of literacy would have daunted less enthusiastic men. They started the Southern Hemisphere Poetry Prize, which was won successively by Herring Lazo, Demetrio Iglesias, Luis Goyeneche Haro, Héctor Cruz and Pablo Sanjuán, among others. They tried to persuade the Chilean Society of Authors, of which they were members, to set up a pension fund for elderly and economically disadvantaged writers, an idea that, given the public's indifference to the problem and the profession's endemic egoism, never got off the ground. Arancibia's literary opus is concentrated in three slim volumes of poetry and a monograph on Pedro González Carrera. His works in a broader sense, fruits of enthusiasm and boundless curiosity, include his legendary voyage through Europe and South Africa in search of the spectral Ramírez Hoffman. Juan Herring Lazo is the author of several poetry collections and plays that were variously received, as well as a trilogy of novels relating the gestation and birth of a new American sensibility based on love. In his final years at the helm of the magazine, he tried to open its pages to virtually all Chilean writers, but fell short of that aim. He was awarded the National Literature Prize. The third editor of the *Southern Hemisphere Literary Review*, Luis Goyeneche Haro, author of ten books of poetry which, viewed as a group, consist simply of variations on the first, tried to follow in Herring Lazo's footsteps, with little success. Under his editorship the magazine went through its most mediocre phase. Pablo Sanjuán, a disciple of Arancibia and a committed fan of González Carrera, tried to change the magazine's direction and steer it back towards the old ideals, while keeping it open to other voices and other ideas, which he sometimes took it upon himself to censor and deform, thereby sparking clashes and quarrels. He tried desperately to make friends, but enemies were all he ever had.

*Steel Garden*. One of the Aryan Brotherhood's magazines.

*Strategy & Tactics*. War games magazine to which Harry Sibelius contributed.

Texan Church of the Last Days. Religious congregation in which Rory Long was a preacher.

*Virginia Wargames*. War games magazine to which Harry Sibelius contributed.

*White Rebels*. One of the Aryan Brotherhood's magazines.

*With Boca*. Magazine founded by Italo Schiaffino. 1976–1983.

The Wounded Eagle. Publishing house founded by Luz Mendiluce.

## 3. BOOKS

*A*, by Zach Sodenstern, Los Angeles, 2013.

*About the Lost Star*, by John Lee Brook, Los Angeles, 1989.

*The Advocate of Cruelty*, by Pedro González Carrera, Santiago, 1980.

*Air Writing*, collection of photographs of Carlos Ramírez Hoffman's aerial poems, published without the author's permission, 1985.

*All My Life*, Edelmira Thompson's first autobiography, Buenos Aires, 1921.

*The Amazons*, by Daniela de Montecristo, Buenos Aires, 1966.

*Ana, the Peasant Redeemed*, by Edelmira Thompson, Buenos Aires, 1935. Opera libretto.

*Anita*, by Zach Sodenstern, Los Angeles, 2010.

*Anthology of the Best Argentinean Jokes*, by Argentino Schiaffino, Buenos Aires, 1972.

*Apocalypse in Force City*, by Gustavo Borda, Mexico City, 1999.

*Apples on the Stairs*, by Jim O'Bannon, Atlanta, 1979.

*Appointed Time*, by Silvio Salvático, Buenos Aires, 1929.

*The Argentinean Horseman*, by Juan Mendiluce, Buenos Aires, 1960.

*Argentinean Hours*, by Edelmira Thompson, Buenos Aires, 1925.

*Argentinean Painting*, by Luz Mendiluce, Buenos Aires, 1959. A torrential 1,500-line poem.

*The Arrival*, by Zach Sodenstern, Los Angeles, 2022. A posthumous novel.

*The Baseball Field*, by Silvio Salvático, Buenos Aires, 1925.

*The Bat Gangsters*, by Zach Sodenstern, Los Angeles, 2004.

*The Best of Argentino Schiaffino*, by Argentino Schiaffino, Buenos Aires, 1989.

*The Best Poems of Jim O'Bannon*, by Jim O'Bannon, Los Angeles, 1990.

*The Birth of New Force City*, by Gustavo Borda, Mexico City, 2005.

*Bitch Luck*, by Silvio Salvático, Buenos Aires, 1923.

*Candace*, by Zach Sodenstern, Los Angeles, 1990.

*Carlota, Empress of Mexico*, by Irma Carrasco. Play premiered at the Teatro Calderón, Mexico City, 1950.

*The Cave Cowboys*, by J.M.S. Hill, New York, 1934.

*Center Forward*, by Silvio Salvático, Buenos Aires, 1927.

*The Century as I Have Lived It*, by Edelmira Thompson in collaboration with Aldo Carozzone, Buenos Aires, 1968.

*The Cephalopods*, by Zach Sodenstern, Los Angeles, 1999.

*Champions*, by Argentino Schiaffino, Buenos Aires, 1978.

*Checking the Maps*, by Zach Sodenstern, Los Angeles, 1993.

*The Children of Jim O'Brady in the American Dawn*, by Jim O'Bannon, Los Angeles, 1993.

*Chimichurri Sauce*, by Argentino Schiaffino, Buenos Aires, 1991.

*Churches and Cemeteries of Europe*, by Edelmira Thompson, Buenos Aires, 1972.

*The Clan of the Bleeding Stigmata*, by J.M.S. Hill, New York, 1929.

*Complete Poems*, by Edelmira Thompson, Buenos Aires, two volumes, 1962 and 1979.

*Complete Poems* I, by Pedro González Carrera, Santiago, 1975.

*Complete Poems* II, by Pedro González Carrera, Santiago, 1977.

*The Confession of the Rose*, by Segundo José Heredia, Caracas, 1958.

*The Conflict of Opposites*, by Luiz Fontaine, Rio de Janeiro, 1939.

*Conversation with Jim O'Brady*, by Jim O'Bannon, Chicago, 1974.

*Correspondence*, by Pedro González Carrera, Santiago, 1982.

*Cosmogony of the New Order*, by Jesús Fernández-Gómez, Buenos Aires, 1977.

*The Countess of Bracamonte*, by Jesús Fernández-Gómez, Cali, 1986.

*Cower, Hounds!* by Italo Schiaffino, Buenos Aires, 1985.

*Crazy Blunders*, by Argentino Schiaffino, Buenos Aires, 1985.

*Creatures of the World*, by Edelmira Thompson, Paris, 1922.

*Cross of Flowers*, by Ignacio Zubieta, Bogotá, 1950.

*Cross of Iron*, by Ignacio Zubieta, Bogotá, 1959.

*Critique of Being and Nothingness*, vol. I, by Luiz Fontaine, Rio de Janeiro, 1955.

*Critique of Being and Nothingness*, vol. II, by Luiz Fontaine, Rio de Janeiro, 1957.

*Critique of Being and Nothingness*, vol. III, by Luiz Fontaine, Rio de Janeiro, 1960.

*Critique of Being and Nothingness*, vol. IV, by Luiz Fontaine, Rio de Janeiro, 1961.

*Critique of Being and Nothingness*, vol. V, by Luiz Fontaine, Rio de Janeiro, 1962.

*The Crystal Cathedral*, by Zach Sodenstern, Los Angeles, 1995.


*Dawn*, by Rory Long, Phoenix, 1972.

*Death Row*, by John Lee Brook, Los Angeles, 1995.

*The Definitive San Martín*, by Carlos Hevia, Montevideo, 1972.

*The Destiny of Pizarro Street*, by Andres Cepeda Cepeda, Arequipa, 1960. Revised and enlarged edition, Lima, 1968.

*The Destiny of Women*, by Irma Carrasco, Mexico City, 1933.

*The Devil's River*, by Mateo Aguirre, Buenos Aires, 1918.

*Diana's Dream*, by Silvio Salvático, Buenos Aires, 1920.

*Don Juan in Havana*, by Ernesto Pérez Masón, Miami, 1979.

*The Doomed Expedition*, by J.M.S. Hill, New York, 1932.


*The Early Saga*, by J.M.S. Hill, New York, 1926.

*The Egotists*, by Juan Mendiluce, Buenos Aires, 1940.

*Les Enfants*, by Edelmira Thompson, Paris, 1922.

*The Enterprise of the Masons*, by Ernesto Pérez Masón, Havana, 1942.

*European Hours*, by Edelmira Thompson, Buenos Aires, 1923.

*Evening in Porto Alegre*, by Luiz Fontaine, Rio de Janeiro, 1964.


*The Fall of Troy*, by J.M.S. Hill, Topeka, 1954.

*Fervor*, by Edelmira Thompson, Buenos Aires, 1985. Juvenilia not included in her *Complete Works*.

*Fields of Honor*, by Silvio Salvático, Buenos Aires, 1936.

*The Fighting Years of an American Falangist in Europe*, by Jesús Fernández-Gómez, Buenos Aires, 1972.

*The Fingerprint Thieves*, by J.M.S. Hill, New York, 1935.

*The First Great Republic*, by Max Kasimir, Port-au-Prince, 1972.

*Footprints on the Beach*, by Silvio Salvático, Buenos Aires, 1922.

*Four Haitian Poets: Mirebalais, Kasimir, Von Hauptman and Le Gueule*, by Max Mirebalais, Port-au-Prince, 1979.
*The Fourth Reich in Denver*, by Zach Sodenstern, Los Angeles, 2002.
*The French Lady*, by Silvio Salvático, Buenos Aires, 1949.

*Geometry*, by Willy Schürholz, Santiago, 1980.
*Geometry II*, by Willy Schürholz, Santiago, 1983.
*Geometry III*, by Willy Schürholz, Santiago, 1984.
*Geometry IV*, by Willy Schürholz, Santiago, 1986.
*Geometry V*, by Willy Schürholz, Santiago, 1988.
*The Gallows Tree*, by Ernesto Pérez Masón, Havana, 1958.
*The Great Buenos Aires Restaurant Novel*, by Argentino Schiaffino, Buenos Aires, 1987.

*Health and Strength*, by Rory Long. Los Angeles, 1984.
*Heartless*, by Ernesto Pérez Mason, Havana, 1930.
*The Horsemen of Repentance*, by Argentino Schiaffino, Miami, 2007.

*Impenitent Memoirs*, by Argentino Schiaffino, 1984.
*Interview with Juan Sauer*, questions and answers probably composed by Carlos Ramírez Hoffman, Buenos Aires, 1979.
*The Invasion of Chile*, by Argentino Schiaffino, Buenos Aires, 1973.
*The Invisible Adorers*, by Carola Leyva, Buenos Aires, 1975. Volume dedicated to Edelmira Thompson; barefaced rehash of Luz Mendiluce's poems.
*The Iron Boat*, by Argentino Schiaffino, Buenos Aires, 1991.
*Iron Youth*, by Argentino Schiaffino, Buenos Aires, 1974.

*Jason's Prize*, by Carlos Hevia, Montevideo, 1989.
*The Jewish Question in Europe*, by Luiz Fontaine, Rio de Janeiro, 1937.
*Juan Diego*, by Irma Carrasco. Play premiered at the Teatro Condesa, Mexico City, 1948.

*Karma Explosion: Wandering Star*, by John Lee Brook, Los Angeles, 1980.
*The Kids*, pornographic novel by Ernesto Pérez Masón published under the pseudonym Abelardo de Rotterdam, New York, 1976.

*The Kids of Puerto Argentino*, by Jorge Esteban Petrovich, Buenos Aires, 1984. A story of imaginary military adventures.
*The Killer's Eyes*, by Silvio Salvático, Buenos Aires, 1962.


*Land of Breezes*, by Max Mirebalais, Port-au-Prince, 1971.
*The Last Canal on Mars*, by J.M.S. Hill, New York, 1934.
*The Last Word*, by Amado Couto, Rio de Janeiro, 1982.
*Life the Way It Is*, by Willy Schürholz under the pseudonym of Gaspar Hauser, Santiago, 1990.
*Like a Hurricane*, by Luz Mendiluce, Mexico City, 1964. Definitive edition, Buenos Aires, 1965.
*Like Wild Bulls*, by Italo Schiaffino, Buenos Aires, 1975.
*A Little House in Napa*, by Zach Sodenstern, Los Angeles, 1987.
*The Lost Ship of Betelgeuse*, by J.M.S. Hill, New York, 1936.
*Luminous Obscurity*, by Juan Mendiluce, Buenos Aires, 1974.


*Macon Night*, by Jim O'Bannon, Macon, 1961.
*Mechanistic Poem*, by Silvio Salvático, Buenos Aires, 1928.
*Meine Kleine Gedichte*, by Franz Zwickau, Caracas, 1982 and Berlin, 1990.
*Memoirs of a Libertarian*, by Ernesto Pérez Masón, New York, 1977.
*The Miracle of Peralvillo*, play by Irma Carrasco, premiered at the Teatro Guadalupe, Mexico City, 1951.
*Montevideo—Buenos Aires*, by Carlos Hevia, Buenos Aires, 1998.
*Motorists*, by Franz Zwickau, Caracas, 1965.
*The Moon in Her Eyes*, play by Irma Carrasco, premiered at the Teatro Principal, Madrid, 1946.
*The Mute Girl*, by Amado Couto, Rio de Janeiro, 1978.
*My Ethics*, by Silvio Salvático, Buenos Aires, 1924.


*Neck in a Noose*, by Curzio Zabaleta, Santiago, 1993.
*Noah's Ark*, by Rory Long, Los Angeles, 1980.
*Nothing to Say*, by Amado Couto, Rio de Janeiro, 1978.
*The New Spring*, by Edelmira Thompson, Buenos Aires, 1931.
*New York Revisited*, by Jim O'Bannon, Los Angeles, 1990.
*Night Signals*, by Segundo José Heredia, Caracas, 1956.

*Occult Poets of Argentina*, anthology of "odd" poetry compiled and annotated by Federico González Irujo, Buenos Aires, 1995.

*The Ostrich*, by Argentino Schiaffino, Buenos Aires, 1988.

*Our Friend B.*, by Zach Sodenstern, Los Angeles, 1996.

*Pain and Image*, by Silvio Salvático, Buenos Aires, 1922.

*The Paradox of the Cloud*, by Irma Carrasco, Mexico City, 1934.

*The Path to Glory*, by Italo Schiaffino, Buenos Aires, 1972.

*Pedrito Saldaña of Patagonia*, by Juan Mendiluce, Buenos Aires, 1970.

"Philosophy of Furniture," by Edgar Allan Poe, *Collected Works*, Cambridge and London, 1978.

*Poems of the Absolute*, by Max Kasimir, Port-au-Prince, 1974.

*Poe's Room*, by Edelmira Thompson, Buenos Aires, 1944. Various editions, a few translations, and a mixed reception. E.T.'s most important work.

*Poor Man's Soup*, by Ernesto Pérez Masón, Havana, 1965.

*The Presidential Summit*, by Argentino Schiaffino, Buenos Aires, 1974.

*Prison Camping*, by Franz Zwickau, Caracas, 1970.

*Railway and Horse*, by Silvio Salvático, Buenos Aires, 1925.

*The Reducers*, by J.M.S. Hill, New York, 1933.

*Refutation of Voltaire*, by Luiz Fontaine, Rio de Janeiro, 1921.

*Refutation of Diderot*, by Luiz Fontaine, Rio de Janeiro, 1925.

*Refutation of D'Alembert*, by Luiz Fontaine, Rio de Janeiro, 1927.

*Refutation of Montesquieu*, by Luiz Fontaine, Rio de Janeiro, 1930.

*Refutation of Rousseau*, by Luiz Fontaine, Rio de Janeiro, 1932.

*Refutation of Hegel, followed by a Brief Refutation of Marx and Feuerbach*, by Luiz Fontaine, Rio de Janeiro, 1938.

*Return to Force City*, by Gustavo Borda, Mexico City, 1995.

*Revolution*, by Zach Sodenstern, Los Angeles, 1991.

*The Rivers and Other Poems*, by Jim O'Bannon, Los Angeles, 1991.

*A Room in the Tropics*, by Max von Hauptman, Paris, 1973. Enlarged edition, Port-au-Prince, 1976.

*The Ruins of Pueblo*, by Zach Sodenstern, Los Angeles, 1998.

*Sad Eyes*, by Silvio Salvático, 1929.

*Saturnalia*, by Segundo José Heredia, Caracas, 1970.

*Seas and Offices*, by Carlos Hevia, Montevideo, 1979.

*Sergeant P.*, by Segundo José Heredia, Caracas, 1955.

*Shadows of Lost Children*, by J. M. S. Hill, New York, 1930.

*The Simbas*, by Zach Sodenstern, Los Angeles, 2003.

*A Simple Philosophy*, by Rory Long, Los Angeles, 1987.

*Sinking Islands*, by Juan Mendiluce, Buenos Aires, 1986. Published posthumously.

*Sleepless Night*, by Silvio Salvático, Buenos Aires, 1921.

*Snow-Trekkers*, by J.M.S. Hill, New York, 1928.

*Solitariness*, by John Lee Brook, 1986.

*Solitude*, by Argentino Schiaffino, Buenos Aires, 1987.

*The Soul of the Waterfall*, by Mateo Aguirre, Buenos Aires, 1936.

*Spain's Gift*, by Irma Carrasco, Madrid, 1940.

*Spectacle in the Sky*, by Argentino Schiaffino, Buenos Aires, 1974.

*Springtime in Madrid*, by Juan Mendiluce, Buenos Aires, 1965.

*The Staircase of Heaven and Hell*, by Jim O'Bannon, Los Angeles, 1986.

*Stale Hearts and Young Hearts*, by Julián Rico Anaya, Buenos Aires, 1978.

*The Storm and the Youths*, by Mateo Aguirre, Buenos Aires, 1911.

*A Story Heard in the Delta*, by Argentino Schiaffino, New Orleans, 2013.

*A Tableau of Volcanoes*, by Irma Carrasco, Mexico City, 1934.

*Talking with America*, by Rory Long, Los Angeles, 1992. Book, audio CD and CD-Rom.

*Tangos of Buenos Aires*, by Luz Mendiluce, Buenos Aires, 1953.

*Terra Autem Erat Inanis*, by Argentino Schiaffino, Buenos Aires, 1996.

*Three Poems to Argentina*, by Silvio Salvático, Buenos Aires, 1923.

*The Time of Argentinean Youth*, a manifesto by Italo Schiaffino, Buenos Aires, 1969.

*A Toast to the Boys*, by Italo Schiaffino, Buenos Aires, 1978.

*A Tranquil Night in Burgos*, play by Irma Carrasco, premiered at the Teatro Principal, Madrid, December 1940.

*To Daddy*, by Edelmira Thompson, Buenos Aires, 1909.

*The Treasure*, by Argentino Schiaffino, Miami, 2010.

*The Triumph of Virtue or the Triumph of God*, by Irma Carrasco, Salamanca, 1939.

*The True Son of Job*, by Harry Sibelius, New York, 1996.

*Twelve*, by Pedro González Carrera, Cauquenes, 1955.

*Unsolved Crimes in Force City*, by Gustavo Borda, Mexico City, 1991.
*Untilled Land*, by Jim O'Bannon, Atlanta, 1971.
*Untitled*, posthumous novel by Zach Sodenstern, Los Angeles, 2023.

*Vindication of John Lee Brook and Other Poems*, John Lee Brook, Los Angeles, 1975.
*The Virgin of Asia*, by Irma Carrasco, Mexico City, 1954.
*The Visitors from Beta Centauri*, J.M.S. Hill, New York, 1928.
*The Voice You Withered*, by Irma Carrasco, Mexico City, 1930.
*Vulture Hill*, by Irma Carrasco, Mexico City, 1952.

*The War Criminals' Son*, by Franz Zwickau, Caracas, 1967.
*Warriors of the South*, by Zach Sodenstern, Los Angeles, 2001.
*The Watchful Eye Club*, by J.M.S. Hill, New York, 1931.
*The Way of the Brave*, by Jim O'Bannon, Atlanta, 1966.
*The Wild World of Roscoe Stuart*, by J.M.S. Hill, New York, 1932.
*Will Kilmartin's Brain in Flames*, by J.M.S. Hill, New York, 1929.
*The Works of T. R. Murchison*, Seattle, 1994. Contains almost all the stories and novels published by Murchison in the various magazines put out by the Aryan Brotherhood.
*The World of Snakes*, by J.M.S. Hill.
*The Witches*, by Ernesto Pérez Masón, Havana, 1940.

*Youthful Ardor*, by Juan Mendiluce, Buenos Aires, 1968.